Christmas On Firefly Hill

GARRETT LEIGH

Praise for Garrett Leigh

"Emotional and brilliant..."

ALL ABOUT ROMANCE

"Tastefully erotic ... more smart than smutty..."

PUBLISHERS WEEKLY

"Powerful and compelling..."

FOREWORD REVIEWS

"An unforgettable voice in every book Leigh writes..." USA
TODAY

For my own bearded superhero <3

Playlist

- Please Come Home For Christmas - *Charles Brown*
- Last Christmas - *Wham!*
- Sleigh Ride - *Carpenters*
- If We Make it Through December - *Pistol Annies*
- Upon A Winter's Night - *Cara Dillon*
- Merry Christmas Baby - *Lou Rawls*
- O Come, All Ye Faithful - *Elvis Presley*
- I'll Be Home For Christmas - *Dean Martin*
- A Spaceman Came Travelling - *Chris de Burgh*
- Stay Another Day - *East 17*
- Carol of the Bells - *John Williams*

Listen on SPOTIFY

Logan

Summer Then

The night is hot and humid, thick August air heavy in the sky. There are no clouds, just smoke trails from the fire show I'm marshalling, the smell of paraffin heady with danger.

I'm not the kind of dude to get excited by that. I flick a scowl at the clear sky. I want it to *rain,* and not just because I'm in a bad mood. This grass, man. It's dry. Yellow. Not far from straw at this point. One spark out of place and this whole field is going up, and because I've seen too much horrible shit to ever believe the worst won't happen, I'm standing here like a doomsday peddler, glaring the heck out of every dancer that spins past.

That's what you get for moonlighting, bro.

My twin brother's amusement is loud in my head, but given his solution to an expensive divorce is playing gangster with a biker crew down south, he can suck a bag.

I'm the sensible one.

Honest.

A fire dancer prances by me, all sequins, flesh, and smoke. She's an attractive woman, but it'd take more than long legs and

1

curves to distract me from hawk-eyeing the flaming staff she twirls.

I don't see her.

I don't see anything but *hazards*.

It's my job.

The woman flits on by. She's last in line and I almost relax. Then an awed murmur ripples through the audience and I remember there's another performer I didn't get to lecture before the show.

Before I even see him, I know he's different. It's not just the louder noise from the festival crowd, it's everything, from the increased heat in the air to the wider expanse of smoke in the sky.

From the goosebumps breaking out over my skin, to the thud of my heart when I finally clap eyes on this fucker.

God*damn*.

There goes my theory about knowing myself.

"You've got a thing for thic brunettes, dude."

Nope. Apparently not. Because there's no way this dude's slender limbs and sunshine-blond hair aren't every sexual thought I've ever had rolled into a fucking thunderbolt.

A *thunderbolt* that hits me straight through the soul.

Like, legit kills me stone dead.

If stones could burn like molten lava, that is.

That's the word for what spreads through me as the dancer whirls closer. He's spinning a flaming poi above his head, a double-ended staff that sends sparks showering all over him as he swings it faster and faster, his nimble body a blur of tattooed skin and that gorgeous fucking hair.

Oh, and he's bare-chested, naturally, dressed in black harem pants that sit low on his narrow hips, the rest of him in full view, from his lean abs right down to his tattooed bare feet.

Fuck me. I might've misjudged my attraction to blonds, but my penchant for the hard planes of a bloke's torso is in full flight. I watch him twist and turn, the dance timeless and primal, and another bolt hits me. Blood rushes south in time with the audible *whoosh* of the poi. In an instant, I'm beside myself with an intensity I haven't felt since a dude first turned my head at the tender age of fifteen.

More than that, because this feeling isn't laced with fear.

This feeling is all fucking heat and I don't have to worry what anyone else thinks about that.

Except maybe anyone within a close enough radius to see the dick print making my utility trousers ridiculously tight.

The only soul close enough is him.

He dances into my peripheral, and *dear lord*, I'm not religious, but I need a divine intervention right now.

I get it in the form of a clap of thunder. A loud whip of sound that breaks the sky open. Raindrops fall, fat and wet. Some of the audience flees. Dancers too. Not this one, though.

Not *him*.

He laughs and turns his face to the inky abyss above us, letting the rain pelt him, soaking his skin.

His poi fizzles out. I wait for his magnetism to fade with it, but as the crowd thins, the aura he carries seems to swell, drawing me in.

I've taken *four* steps before I catch myself, and by then it's too late.

He sees me and lowers the poi, a grin stretching a face I'm fast realising is a thousand suns more beautiful than his bewitching body. Drumbeats still come from the band beneath the boho umbrellas. They thud an ancient rhythm in time with my heart. I take two more steps. We're inches apart, and up close, his smile is blinding.

And older than I expect. Mid-twenties rather than the nineteen-year-old I feared he might be with flexibility like that.

Older and *fucking hell*, he's stunning. All cheekbones and hair. It's too dark to see what colour his eyes are, but they could be mud-brown and he'd still, hands down, be the most beautiful man I've ever seen.

He's also waiting for me to speak, and I realise, too late, I have nothing to say that isn't various versions of *I want to fuck you*. And I can't say that—I'm working. And shy, at least when it comes to picking up men. I'm a damn good lay, and I know it, but this bit...yeah. I'm ten shades of terrible.

A silence stretches out. It should be awkward, but he's still moving to the primal drumming, like it's part of him, swaying his hips, head bobbing. He reaches out and flips the crew ID hanging from a lanyard around my neck.

"Logan Halliwell," he breathes. "You're a fire marshal."

I nod.

He tilts his head, his big eyes slightly hazed from the zoot I spot between his fingers. "Did I do something wrong?"

"No—" My voice is as croaky as his is warm and melodic. I try again. "*No.* Just checking you're okay. You had sparks all over you."

I itch to grab his wrists and check his skin. His inked chest, neck, and hands. The tattoos are chakras and mandalas, in thick black-blue ink that didn't come from a modern tattoo gun. They're imperfectly perfect, like the glowing copper pendant hanging from his elegant neck, and I want to trace them with my tongue.

"I'm good."

His voice startles me. I drag my eyes from his chest to meet the snare of his gaze. "Good?"

"Yeah." He draws the word out, then takes a toke from the joint, blowing the herbal smoke sideways from his lush mouth. "I'm used to it. Probably wouldn't notice if I lit myself on fire."

"That's what I'm here for."

"You gonna save me?"

Save him. Toss him over my shoulder and carry him to my fucking cave. "I'd try."

4

"That's nice of you."

"I'm a nice man."

"You look it."

Can't say I've ever been told that before. I'm big and wide, my hair as dark as my brother's is light. He says I have a grumpy mug, and no one's ever told me any different. "You look—" Fuck. How am I gonna finish that sentence? With the truth? Nah. My internal monologue is articulate as shit, but put me in front of someone who makes my heart skip like a broken clock and my tongue sticks to the roof of my mouth. "You look all right too."

Amazing. At this rate, we'll be married by the end of the month.

Not.

Besides, I'm not in the market for another expensive clusterfuck. I'm down to fuck. I just don't know how to say it without sounding like a colossal wanker.

So I don't say it. I say nothing else at all, and neither does he. We stand in the rain and stare at each other until someone behind me calls my name.

It's the festival organiser. She's a nice lady paying me cash for a couple of days' work, but dear god I wish I'd never met her right now.

If you'd never met Xena you wouldn't be kicking it in this wet field.

Can't argue with that, but if she's calling my name, she needs me for something, and that means stepping out of the vortex this dude has sucked me into with an angelic smile that somehow holds the heat of the devil.

He steps closer. "Someone wants you."

It's a whisper my dick chooses to take out of context. *I want you.* It's not what he said. Not even close. But I hear it, bank it, and steel myself to turn away from him.

A hand skates over my hip, scalding fingers grazing my skin

through the thin T-shirt I resent even more than Xena for calling my name a second time.

The dancer leans in.

I catch the scent of accelerants and smoke, a hair trigger for hyper-vigilance on any normal day or night. But there's nothing normal about the rush his proximity gives me. Nothing about it I don't like, save the fact I know I'm about to lose it.

His hand on my hip burns me up. Scrambles my brain. I meet him halfway, but I've got nothing. I don't know what I'm doing. What *he's* doing. Where we're going.

I have no clue that his hot-as-hell mouth is about to land on mine, so when it does I'm a fucking statue. A fortress of nothing as his hot lips brush mine in a sweet ghost of a kiss.

He's kissing me.

Ten years ago, the mere idea of a man's kiss in a public place was enough to give me a fucking stroke. Now it's a different kind of trip. One that spins me in the best ways, lifts me off my feet, and takes me on a magic carpet ride.

His lips are everything.

Then they're gone and I realise I've stone-faced him.

Scared him, probably. Mean mug, remember?

He doesn't look scared.

He looks amused. *Joyfully* amused and my lips begin to rise. Another clap of thunder rattles the earth and I make my move, tugging him back into my orbit.

I kiss him. In front of hundreds of festival goers. In front of Xena, and every dancer still braving the rain. Lightning flashes in the sky and it's fitting with the chemical combustion happening in my body with every soft flex of my mouth on his.

It's funny how the world can shift in a split second. I mean, that's how long I kiss him for. Seconds. No tongues or teeth, just gentle lips. But by the time it's over, I'm a different person.

A better person, maybe. I don't know.

All I know for certain is that I have to go as much as I want to stay, and he knows it, too. I see it in eyes that still have no colour.

He steps back.

I let him go.

He dances away with his lips imprinted on mine forever.

Remy

Winter Now

Early mornings have always spoken to me. Cold and wet. Hot and dry. I don't mind. Even the grey ones lift my spirits. The mist. The rain. Doesn't matter if I've been awake all night, trying to get comfortable on the sagging mattress in the back of my beat-up Transit, it still feels brand new.

I don't even mind the melting frost seeping through my battered boots. I'll be cursing my damp socks later, but right now the sparkly ground at the foot of Firefly Hill is magical enough to distract me from the fact it'll be spring before I can afford new boots, and who knows when I'll get my socks dry.

That could all change today. I close my eyes briefly, leaning on the back doors of my van, testing my state of mind to see if I feel lucky. Nope. Not really. But there's a lump of peridot in my pocket. Maybe that'll help.

Something has to. I'm a humble bloke. I don't need much. But winter in my van is killing me. There's tightness in my chest from the damp, and the bones I broke in the middle of the festival season have this dull throb I can't shift.

I'm tired. Probably. In the summer months, I love my van. The freedom. The great outdoors. But the colder it gets, the harder it is to sleep. Not just because it's freezing, but because I'm scared and pissed off, emotions I've spent most of my life fortunate enough to avoid.

The sun rises behind the hill, bathing the scattered dwellings with a misty glow. It's not exactly tropical, but I soak up the faint warmth while eyeing the path I need to take later this morning, up the winding road to the highest house on the peak. Behind it is a building I can't see from below, a concrete-walled workshop that could save my life. I can't afford the rent up front, or even a deposit, so I'm relying on my charm.

And the fact I managed to sneak a shower at a fucking *glacial* waterfall last night. I might be frozen to the marrow, but I'm clean.

I'm not meeting my potential new landlord until midmorning. It's barely dawn, but I need to get moving before I seize up. Mentally. Physically. I'm not good at staying still. So I walk into town, ignoring the low thrum of pain in my hip. The quiet thump in my shoulder. Sitting around feels like waiting to die, and I'm not there yet.

I have too much to do. Besides, this place is too pretty for me to sulk once I get here. It's November, but the Christmas fairies have been busy. There are lights everywhere, street art, and ad posters for festive performances. The air even carries cinnamon and spice, but I'm pretty sure the coffee shop smells the same all year round.

Like heaven in a paper cup.

I have two quid in my pocket. Truth be told, I need to buy some instant rice and a banana for my dinner, but coffee, man. I want it. I *need* it. And I'm not always good at long-term thinking. If I was, there's a chance I wouldn't be living in a van in darkest winter, scraping pocket change together for the smallest Americano this town has to offer.

Hot coffee helps me not ride that train of thought too hard. I take my precious cup to the park on the outskirts of suburbia.

It has the best views. From the bench where I slouch I can see the whole town and the landscape beyond, where the hills and fields give way to the industry in the distance. The big city with its twinkly lights and high-rises.

I like cities when I'm far away from them. When I can talk myself into the promise of the unknown. Bright lights and opportunity. From up here, it's easy to forget it's full of shit I don't want. Give me a tent in a field. A burning poi in my hands. The summer sun unimpeded by plastic and litter.

Right. Because there's no litter at festivals. Or doped-up dickheads who nearly killed you.

I sigh and drain my coffee. The bitter tension in my gut is an unwelcome intruder. I squash it down, but it leaves an itchy feeling in its wake. I need to move again, but I have nowhere to go, unless I want to traipse back to the van and catch a nap before I hike up a hill to meet a man I've been told goes by the name of Uncle Marr.

A snooze sounds good. But I have form for sleeping through every method I employ to wake me when my time is up. Also, I want to be tired. Chasing exhaustion gives me more chance of sleeping tonight and I need that more than anything.

So I stay where I am, watching early-morning joggers, commuters heading for the station, and school children playing on the frost-damp play apparatus while their parents tell them not to. It's a nice scene, almost as good as a nap, and I find myself drifting, eyes growing heavy, muscles relaxing. The pain in my aching bones fades and it's all I can do to stay awake.

I'm on my way to failure when a new family arrives. A father with two boys. Twins, I realise. Identical in everything except their personalities. The kid in the red hat is running towards the climbing wall, his gap-toothed grin a mile wide. His brother is wearing blue and shuffling along next to his dad, kicking stones and chewing his lip.

He doesn't want to climb the wall. My guess is he'd rather

be indoors with the Ironman figure he's carrying in the hand that isn't clutching his dad's, but he keeps shuffling on anyway, only stopping when he comes to the foot of the structure his brother is already halfway up. He tilts his head to look and his chin starts to wobble. He's a cute kid and it breaks my heart, but he's got a good dad. A kind one, so tall and strong he has to squat down to talk to his son.

I try not to stare, but it's tough. The kid's dad has his back to me, but wow, what a back. He's wearing a long-sleeved tee over old jeans and scuffed boots. No coat, as if he's impervious to the cold that's creeping into every part of me. His shoulders are thick and broad, and even from this distance I can tell he's roped with muscle. The kind a man gets from an honest day's graft.

He wraps his big hands around his boy's tiny ones. I can't see his face or what I'm guessing is his chiselled jaw moving, but I can tell by the kid's face that his dad is speaking to him. Soothing him. Reassuring him.

A moment later, the other kid hops down from the wall and mimics his father's pose. His face is serious, drawn in a manly frown too old for his young face, and it makes me smile. The last thing I ever wanted to do was be like my dad, but for this kid I can tell it's the ultimate endgame.

Cute.

So cute, I have to look away, from Big Daddy, at least. Remembering the last time dark hair and broad shoulders stole my attention is a dangerous preoccupation, and there's nothing hotter to me than a man who isn't afraid to be nice.

I like nice.

Greenfest dude was nice. You told him so.

That I did. And I kissed him. Two weeks to the day before my entire life crashed to earth, but I'm not in the mood to think about that. Or to have filthy thoughts about a man I'll probably never see again. With another soul-breaking sigh, I fire my empty cup at a nearby bin, and drag myself on my merry way.

Uncle Marr is exactly as I pictured him. Ancient and crusty, with nicotine-stained fingers and a gaze so sharp I'm worried he's going to slit me open and see the bullshit inside.

Not that I'm giving him any bullshit. I'd been in his company point-two seconds when I realised there was no point.

Besides, bullshit isn't my style. It's hard work and why bother when the truth is shitty enough? "I can't pay you anything until I fill the orders on my books. And I can't do that without a functional workshop."

Marr rolls a cigarette with his thumb and finger, regarding me with yellowed eyes. "What is this business you're in? My missus said it was jewellery."

"It is, among other things. I make stuff with old coins. Copper, mainly."

"Copper? Like pennies?"

I nod. "It's free money. People chuck it in skips instead of taking it to the bank."

Marr is old enough that he can see the madness in that. But we're living in different times to the ones that shaped him. Disposable, man. Everything's disposable.

Even you.

Especially me.

Marr still looks confused. I dig my phone from my pocket and the pendant under my clothes "This is the style of jewellery I make. And I have orders for the tabletops and the lamps, but nowhere to make them. If I can get my head down for the next few weeks, I can pay you three months' rent by mid-December."

And then some, if I'm lucky. But despite the peridot in my pocket, that word hasn't been my friend in recent months, and I steel myself for rejection. For the derisive laughter that chased me out of the last unit I tried to rent.

Marr surprises me with open curiosity. He takes my phone and peers at it. Then wraps his weathered fingers around the shiny penny at my neck. "How'd you make this then?"

"With a drill, a mandrel, and some other bits. Some of it, I can do from my van when the weather's good, but I need space for the blowtorch and the bigger pieces. Dry storage too."

"You got all that? The tools and materials?"

I nod and swipe my phone screen, showing him a picture of the packed interior of the Transit, the mattress hidden behind the heavy oak I need to lay with shiny copper pennies by the end of next week. "I just need space, man."

"It's cold in here."

I know that. Draughty too. But it's dry at the top of Firefly Hill, I can taste it in the clean air. This place is perfect for me. I just need Uncle Marr to give me a chance.

The old man goes back to studying my wares. I lift the leather from around my neck, hand it over, and give him some room to think.

I wander around the workshop that's more an outbuilding than anything else, with some aged workbenches that have seen better days, a burner, and a tiny utility room with a toilet and basin. It smells of wood and dust. Of old paint and stale varnish. It calls to my heart, and I love it. But there's a deeper connection too, one I usually only feel when I'm barefoot in the forest. *Or locking eyes with handsome fire marshals, daring them to kiss you back.*

Bloody hell. The thought of that charged summer kiss makes me smile again, like it always does. A precious memory I'll never let go. Happy things are hard to recall sometimes, but his lips on mine comes to me as easy as breathing. How soft they were in contrast with the scratch of his unshaven jaw on my cheek. The sweet taste of mint. His gentle grin against my mouth and how it lit his entire burly self right up.

I see that smile in my dreams sometimes, more than I feel his kiss. More than I picture what might've happened if he hadn't been called away and the truck I'd rolled into Greenfest on hadn't rolled right back out to perform elsewhere.

God, I wish he'd fucked me. Then some days I'm glad he didn't. My imagination is wild and I like it that way. Keeps me company when it's too cold and lonely to get any sleep.

"Is nice this. Might get one for the missus if you come good."

I startle and spin around. Despite the messy urgency I carried up the hill, Uncle Marr's presence has slipped my mind. He's holding up the pendant, frowning at the aged leather I've had around my neck since I was fourteen, watching the copper dance in the sunlight filtering through the dusty windows.

Hope feels like a stranger, but I'm good at embracing the positive. I let it plant careful seeds, and return to Marr's side. "She'd probably want something more delicate. Like this." I show him a photo on my Etsy page. The penny is shaved smaller and threaded onto a chain. "I can engrave them too. Or cut them to specific shape, like a moon and stars, animals. Whatever you want."

I swipe through more pictures, wishing I had a bigger screen for his old eyes. But whatever he sees seems to please him. He settles on a rose design, with the penny set within a gemstone of green aventurine. I tell him, "Aventurine signifies serenity, wisdom, and power."

Marr sniffs. "Sounds about right. Just don't go putting them ideas in her head. She's a tyrant as it is. How much you knocking these out for?"

"This one? Fifty quid. But I'll do it for nothing if you'll give me a six-month lease."

Marr mulls it over and I force myself to remain still while he does. I want to look out of the window. Peek at the cottage fifty feet below me, where his nephew lives with his family and *"keeps an eye on things."* When he'd said that, it had felt like a threat, but now there's light at the end of this—*possible light*—I'm intrigued more than anything. I like people. I like kids and families and everything that comes with it. Who knows? Maybe I'll make a new friend.

"I'll give you a year."

I blink again. Marr is looming over me, counting tenners out of a wallet as old as he is. "A year?"

He nods and hands me fifty quid. "I can't be doing with chopping and changing tenants every few months. Rather let the place rot, but the boy won't have it."

"The boy?"

Marr jerks his head at the door. "My nephew. Thinks he can boss me about."

I feel like I'm floating. I have money in my hand and the prospect of a whole year in a place that's already making my blood move faster around my body, oiling the parts rusted by an autumn of misery. "You don't have to pay me for your wife's necklace."

Marr rebuffs my attempt to hand the money back. "Go on with you. How are you going to pay your rent if you're already giving your goods away?"

He's entirely serious, but I can't contain the grin that rises from my belly and splits my face in half.

Marr almost smiles back at me. He holds out a hand for me to shake while sticking his rollie between his lips with the other. "Last year I gave the missus a cactus and she weren't happy. As long as you save me from another coating like that, we'll be grand. The boy handles the money. He'll be round later to iron out the details."

Just like that, it's done. Marr eases a flat cap over his bald head and shuffles out of the workshop. Out of *my* workshop.

Then he's gone and I'm alone with dreams and aspirations that have a shot at coming true.

It's a giddy feeling till I remember I have to traipse back down the hill to fetch my van. The Transit is a rusted heap of shit. I didn't drive it up here in case my new landlord thought I was a tramp.

Now it's raining like hell and I'm realising Uncle Marr wouldn't have given a shit either way.

Logan

Food shop day is the bane of my week. Of my existence, actually. Least that's how it feels on the back of a brutal night shift.

My skin smells of chemical smoke. It's bitter and acrid, and I bite down on my molars as I get a whiff of it reaching for the vegetables no fucker is gonna eat.

I buy them so my ex-wife thinks I'm someone I'm not. As if she doesn't know me or our boys haven't swallowed anything green in years. Like a broccoli or two is going to make me a better man than the one she left.

Idiot. Times a thousand. I add cabbage too, because it keeps for weeks and puts off this charade for as long as possible, then I make my escape to the meat aisle, rubbing my gritty eyes as I stare at the vac packs of protein and cholesterol.

This bit is easier, but no less ridiculous. I pile bacon and sausages into my trolley. Drumsticks and chops. It's almost funny that I think I'll have motivation to cook any of it when I haven't rustled up more than beans on toast since a week last Sunday, but I throw it all in anyway.

I'm loading up on tinned soup, Pot Noodles, and spaghetti

hoops when my phone explodes in a cacophony of noise I'm unprepared for.

Billy changed my ringtone again.

To the Imperial march from *Star Wars*.

For his mother's contact.

Cheers, son. I dig the phone from my back pocket and wedge it between my chin and my shoulder, still half engrossed in the Heinz selection. "Bec."

"Lo." She says my name with a smile in her voice. Despite the conflict we often find ourselves in, she likes me, and I like her. That was never the problem. "Boys get into school okay?"

"Sam left a shoe in the car. Had to drop it off when I found it ten minutes down the road. Other than that it was pretty seamless."

"He made it from the car to the classroom with one shoe before anyone noticed?"

"It was his PE plimsol thing. I'm not that shit."

"Never said you were."

There it is. The tension that bleeds between us when we're not on our best behaviour.

I sigh and move on to the snack aisle, the one place I know I'm not going to fuck everything up. Bec's talking to me about pick-up times and washing school uniforms. I'm listening, I take it all in, but I'm too damn tired to contribute much.

"You won't forget, will you?"

I pause with my hand on a Doritos multipack. "Hmm?"

"For god's sake, Lo. Are you even present right now?"

"How present do you want me to be? I just got off a fucking night shift and you're bending my ear about shit we've already arranged."

"I'm not bending your ear. I'm reminding you that I'm leaving for that exhibition on Sunday morning. So you need to pick the boys up for football."

"What time?"

"The same time as always."

"Eleven?"

Bec's irritation crackles down the line. If I close my eyes, I can see her all too clearly, pacing her studio, long nails tapping the back of her phone case. "That's when it finishes. You need to pick them up from here at eight-thirty and take them to the pavilion. And for once in your life don't be late."

That stings. And it's not fair. "You know I can't promise that. I'm on the overnight."

"You have to promise," Bec snaps. "Why is your job more important than mine?"

"I'm a firefighter. It's not my—"

"Yeah, yeah. I know. You're a hero. I've heard it all before, and I don't care, okay? I don't *care*. I need you to show up, Lo. For real. I need you to show up for them and for me. If you can't, then we need to start thinking about other arrangements."

She hangs up without elaborating. And I don't need her to. The *other arrangements* are her taking our boys and moving three counties away to where her boyfriend lives. So he can pick my kids up from school. Take them to football on Sundays. Cook them bad dinners and watch Marvel films with them while Bec exhibits her weird as fuck artwork all over the damn world.

So she can *upgrade* me to a better model.

I throw the Doritos into the trolley hard enough that Billy will be trailing cheese dust all over the house, but I don't give a shit. I like the dust. I like the mess and the noise, because I love *them*. My kids. My boys. I'd die if they weren't here.

Trouble is, fighting fires is all I'm good at. And I need the money, given that Bec left every part of our marriage behind, including the debts and the mortgage.

Fuck's sake. I load up on Christmas-themed biscuits and stomp to the checkout, glowering at the dude on the till and his glittery festive jumper. I'm at the car when my phone goes again. Grumpy as hell, I ignore it. Bec has form for rinse and repeat phone calls and I'm not in the mood. I have five hours before I pick the boys up. Five hours to clean the house, wash the clothes, and get some sleep before my patience deserts me enough to say something I'll regret.

The call rings out.

A few minutes later comes the a beep of a voicemail message. *Not Bec then*.

I'm all out of heavy sighs. I slam the boot shut and slide behind the wheel before I retrieve my phone and see my batshit uncle's name on the screen.

Calling him back is a river I can't cross right now. I tap into the voicemail instead and listen to him ramble on about gas prices and overheads. I'm out of town by the time he gets to the point. There's a new tenant in the workshop he owns up the hill from my house. A tenant who's paying no rent until Christmas but he still wants me to go and talk to about money that has fuck all to do with me.

Awesome.

My bad mood lays down fresh roots. I drive home and follow a battered Transit up the hill to Firefly Cottage. It's moving slowly, like anyone who doesn't know the road as well as I do. I've seen too many horrible car wrecks to be too annoyed about it, but I'm annoyed all the same. Restless, drumming my fingers on the wheel of my own ancient vehicle. I need to text my uncle back before he rings me again. I need to do something with the slow cooker and the mountain of chicken drumsticks I've brought home.

I *need* to wash the smoke scent from my skin and shut my damn eyes for longer than a dazed blink.

The Transit rumbles all the way to my house and keeps going, hitting the dirt track that leads nowhere but the workshop at the top of the hill. Logic tells me it's the new tenant and I'm not particularly interested in whatever loon Uncle Marr has recruited to make copper jewellery in my back garden, but my gaze follows the van anyway.

It slows to a crawl on the unlaid road, taking the steep curve with enough caution that I should look away and leave them to it, but I'm trapped in a haze of fatigue. A foggy stare that won't quit.

The rusty van makes it to the top of the hill and reverse parks, bringing the rear of the vehicle to the workshop's rolling garage door. The engine shuts off and I realise how loud it was. My Discovery is twenty years old, but this heap of junk is prehistoric. And, if I'm being honest, cool as fuck. It has mismatched paint, and magic mushrooms etched on the bonnet.

It makes me wonder what kind of old hippie is driving it. My uncle is a magnet for the weird and wonderful. The last tenant was a woman who wove her own clothes from bamboo and yarn.

I sit back in my seat, taking the keys from the ignition but making no move to get out. Left to my own devices, I could sleep right here, but there's ice cream in the boot, so I force my heavy eyes to stay open.

The driver of the Transit opens the door and slides out. From this distance, I can't see much, save that it's a dude. A slim one who favours his right leg as he hops down from the van and moves to the back.

He has narrow shoulders and blond hair. A grace in his step, despite the fact he's limping a little. I can't see his face, but somehow there's a tug in my chest I haven't felt since early summer, when I laid my lips on that ethereal fire dancer I still see in my dreams, dirty and sweet. I've resigned myself that nothing will ever come close to whoever that was, but something about this man's lithe build and rain-damp hair feels familiar enough that I know I'm delirious.

21

I need to sleep. I can't fight it anymore. I'm done.

Unpacking the food shop is a hell pit I can't face. I retrieve the ice cream, chicken, and fish fingers and leave the rest where it is.

My footsteps are heavy on the wet ground. I hear the slam of a van door. It jolts me, that pull in my chest flaring to life. But I don't turn round. I push on, dump my wares and my boots, and pass out on the couch.

I don't sleep well. Never do on the sofa. Like everything else, including how I feel, it's old and lumpy, and despite some nostalgic summer dreams that put a smile on my face, I wake with a jump and a crick in my neck ten minutes before I have to drive back into town to fetch the boys from school.

After the quickest shower known to man, I make it to the school gates with seconds to spare.

Billy whizzes out like he has a rocket up his arse.

Sam is slower, his face solemn, thumb jammed in his mouth. He's seven. Too old for me to scoop into my arms now, but god, I want to.

I crouch to his level and tug his thumb free of his mouth. "What's up, little man?"

He shrugs, not one for talking unless we're at home and he's excited about something. Those are the moments I live for. The rare moments when my shy kid won't shut the hell up. But we're a long way from that right now. "Are we sleeping at your house tonight?"

"Yup. That okay with you?"

"What's for dinner?"

"Why? You gonna ditch me if I bosh out chip butties again?" I tweak his chin to let him know I'm not serious. About him ditching me, at least. Can't promise I won't swing by the chippy on the way home.

Sam thinks on his answer, but he's cut off by his rowdy brother.

Billy yanks on my sleeve. "Can we go to the park again?"

He's an adrenaline junkie. He wants to scale the climbing wall and leap from the top, pretending he can fly. But as much I love to see him happy, I have a million and one things to do at home. "Not today, bud. We can ride the bikes, though, if you do your reading super quick."

That's not going to happen. Getting Billy to read is like pulling teeth from a stubborn walrus. An affronted frown settles on his freckled face and we set off for home.

At this point, the drive from town to the summit of Firefly Hill is a journey I can make in my sleep. Sometimes, I'm half convinced I do.

We're home before I know it, and I find my gaze drawn to the Transit van again before Billy hits the back of my head with a plastic airplane.

"Hey." I reach back and wrench it from his hand. "Watch what you're doing with that thing."

"You were supposed to catch it."

"Warn your old dad next time, eh?"

"I did, duh."

I give him a look to let him know talking to me like that will get him in trouble next time I'm energetic enough to give a shit.

He doesn't give a shit, and he hops out of the car.

Away from the school gates, putting Sam on my shoulders is a no-brainer. His laugh makes every ache and pain of my nap on the couch worth it.

I carry him to the front door. "Duck, kiddo. Unless you want to leave your brains outside."

We make it indoors without any decapitations. The boys scamper off in fear of me asking them to clean something. It's amazing how fast they can disappear when they want to. How quiet Billy can be when he's avoiding picking up all his crap from the bedroom floor.

I don't mind. The mess pisses Bec off, but I like it. It reminds me they exist when I'm here on my own.

Could do without the empty fridge, though. Then I remember I went shopping and the next half hour of my life belongs to putting it away.

I throw tins and packets into cupboards and turn the oven on.

Billy appears as I'm shaking oven chips onto a tray and buttering bread. "Fish fingers or Dippers?"

"Dippers. With beans, not peas."

"I didn't buy any peas."

"Cos you're the best dad."

"I'm your only dad. Why are you being nice? You want something?"

Billy sidles further into the kitchen and attempts to climb the cabinets to sit on the counter, but it's too high for him. I'm a big dude, but my kids are slight like their mum, and still catching up from their premature birth.

I hoist Billy onto the counter and lean down so we're eye level. "What are you after?"

He chews on his lip, a tell more characteristic of his twin brother.

He's nervous.

Fuck that.

I soften my expression, all too aware my resting bitch face is an angry bear who needs a cigarette. *You don't smoke anymore.*

Shame. "Come on now." I wipe something unidentified and sticky from my son's face. "Spit it out. I won't bite."

"We have to make model farms for our home project. Mum says you have to do it this time because she's too busy."

Fuck's sake. "Model farms? Made from what?"

"Anything. Like a shoe box and grass or something, I dunno."

"When?"

24

"Before the nativity."

"When's that?"

"It's in the letter Mum gave you."

I abandon Billy and move to the fridge where all the school letters Bec shoves in my face are secured by a magnet. Sure enough, the model farm letter is right there with a heart shaped Post-It stuck to the top, a sweet note from my ex-wife scrawled on the pink paper.

It's your turn to face the consequences of our mutant copulation.

An exasperated chuckle escapes me. Bec's always jokingly held me responsible for the double trouble our lives revolve around. Doesn't matter how many times I explain the biology. That twins run on the *maternal* side and it's a freakish coincidence that I'm a twin too.

I go back to Billy with the letter. "We haven't got long, and I'm on shift more than half of the time we do have, so if you've got any bright ideas, speak them now."

He doesn't. Billy likes being outside and being loud. Sam's the one who's good with his hands, but when I find him he's too engrossed in the X-Box to give a shit.

I wrestle him away from it, feed my kids a Birds Eye special, then we sack off reading practice and chase the fading light to the garage to fetch our push bikes.

The boys are good riders and Firefly Hill is as safe as it gets to let them go. They tear off towards the copse where the ramps are. I follow, ready to scrape them up if they tumble.

They don't.

Not this time.

They ride the jumps over and over, only stopping when I tell them it's getting too dark for me to see them.

I don't let them ride the dirt track back to the house at night. No one ever drives up here except my uncle, the postman, and his random tenants, but I keep my boys close on the way home. Make them wheel their bikes and walk.

"Who's that?" Sam stops and points up the hill.

I follow his gaze to the workshop. The big door is open and the dude I saw earlier is bent over a slab of oak, his back to us as he sands it down, his slim frame as alluring as it was earlier.

His hair is dry now, wavy and blond.

Messy.

I try not to stare too hard.

Fail.

Takes me a second to remember Sam's question. "It's Gruncle's new tenant."

"What's his name?"

"No idea."

It suddenly feels imperative that I find out. I take two steps towards the workshop before I catch myself. *What are you doing?*

The answer is simple: I'm introducing myself to my uncle's tenant so it isn't awkward as hell when I have to take money from him at some far-off point in the future.

But it's more than that, and I can't explain it. I'm beyond curious. I'm *captivated*. And I don't know why. I've never seen this dude's face.

Goddamn, twelve hours ago, I didn't know he existed.

So why am I pushing my bike uphill to change that when my kids need a bath and I need some alone time with my bed?

My brain produces no sensible answers.

So we shove on and ascend the brow of Firefly Hill in time for the mystery man to slide from his work stool and move further into the shop.

His limp is less pronounced now. If I wasn't staring so hard my eyeballs are in danger of popping out of my damn head, I probably wouldn't notice.

As it is, I watch his left leg move too slow for the rest of him and choke on a wave of nosiness that makes no fucking sense.

Maybe living on nuggets and chips is bad for you, bro.

I silence my twin. Locke thinks he's hilarious, but in moments like these, when I *really* need his calming presence in my life, his pseudo jokes are annoying enough that I want to rage text him for something he hasn't actually said.

Also, I kind of agree with the version of my brother that lives, rent-free, in my head. I need more in my life than frozen food and deathly fires.

I also need to follow through with the mad dash I've made up the hill, preferably before Transit Dude disappears.

The boys dump their bikes and come to my side. I dismount and lean mine against the side of the workshop. Then I knock on the metal garage door that's half raised. "Hello?"

For a second, there's no verbal response. Then footsteps come closer and tatty boots appear at the bottom of faded cotton harem pants that are sexy as hell, but pretty terrible at keeping a man warm in the gale blowing up the hill.

You can't find a dude sexy when you haven't seen his face.

Watch me. Besides, I'm about to see his face. The boots come closer and tattooed hands reach for the door. Chakras. Mandalas. Tiny trees across his knuckles that send my heart into this flip that makes me feel unhinged.

The door starts to raise, but it's old and it sticks, and the muttered curse I hear makes my breath catch in my throat.

I know that voice.

No. *No.* I don't. The voice I hear is one I've imagined so many times, awake and asleep, that it bears no resemblance to reality. Obsession doesn't make fact. If it did, the heat rising in my blood would have somewhere to go. A purpose beyond an inevitable and tortured wank in the shower later.

As it is, my brain feels as rusted and stuck as this damn door.

It was one kiss. Stop using it as an excuse to be a fucked up human.

Irritated, I reach for the aged metal and give it a shove. It budges an inch. It's not enough, but it'll do.

I duck under in the same moment the man on the other side does the same. We meet in the middle, half stooped, heads almost clashing. I catch a lungful of woodsmoke and copper. Then eyes the colour of coffee beans ensnare me, wide, beautiful, and framed with chocolate lashes and golden brows.

High cheekbones.

Sunshine-blond hair.

The scruffy jaw is new, but goddamn, it's the face of my dreams. It's the *man* of my dreams, and his grin is fucking blinding.

Remy

I've had enough good fortune today that the sight of the hulking strap of loveliness ducking beneath the workshop door is a step too far.

His face is familiar, of course it is—his sea-green eyes and inky hair. The tousled dark locks that frame his regal bone structure. Even though he's missing the beard from the summer, he looks like Rollo from *Vikings*, but bigger, and a thousand times prettier.

He's also real, despite the unwelcome cynic I've carried for the past few months telling me it can't be so.

Real, and stooped at the most awkward angle ever for a man of his size.

I forgot how tall he is.

It's the sole thought in my head as I retreat and straighten, pulling myself back into the workshop.

I half expect him to disappear. To evaporate in a haze of no sleep and not enough food. But he follows, filling the space in front of me and gifting me the first unimpeded and unimagined view of him since way back when.

Bloody hell, he's gorgeous.

And confused. Whatever this place is to him, I'm the last

person he expected to find here. It's obvious by the divot between his dark brows and the way his jaw seems set in stone.

I'm struck dumb too, but I recover quicker, and a wider smile splits my face. "Fancy seeing you here."

His eyebrow twitches. *Logan's* eyebrow. I remember from that night—from his ID, and the woman who called his name and stole him from me. The festival organiser, but I saw the way she'd looked at him. The way *everyone* had looked at him as he'd walked away from me with my kiss on his lips.

He's stop-traffic beautiful and he has no idea.

He's also as tongue-tied as he was that night, raising his big hand to rub his mouth, as if it's a genie's lamp that'll gift him the right words to say.

I wait a moment longer before I help him out. "Remy. From Greenfest. Though you probably don't recognise me with all my clothes on."

Logan's answer is a startled laugh, but it breaks the tension and he holds out his hand. The one that touched his lips. Maybe that's why the second his warm palm touches mine I feel a charge that vanquishes every lonely ache in my body.

I want to touch his lips too, but I contain myself better than I did that first night.

One: I'm sober.

Two: I'm not so entranced by him that I haven't noticed the little feet waiting for him outside.

Logan's still not speaking. I force myself to release his hand and peer beneath the broken garage door.

Two cute faces stare back.

Two *identical* faces, and it dawns on me that not only is Logan the sweetest kiss I've ever had, he's also the daddy bear from the park this morning.

Holy hell. *Am I even alive right now?*

Cos it feels like I've died and gone to heaven.

I grin at the kids. The climber grins back. The quieter one

takes an alarmed step behind his brother and Logan moves too, I feel him close the narrow distance between us and lean down beside me.

He holds out the hand that was wrapped around mine a second ago. Says nothing verbally, but I watch him connect with his children. Sense that shit, and it's everything.

They come to him. The climber has a curious gaze that pins on me the second he crosses the threshold. The shy one hides behind Logan's legs. Muscled legs still encased in the jeans he was wearing this morning.

The same long-sleeved tee hides his body from me too, clinging to his broad shoulders, his veined forearms on show as if it's not two degrees outside. "These your kids?"

I already know they are—they're his mirror image in everything but size—but getting Logan to talk to me has become my number one priority. I *need* him to talk to me to tie me down to a world that has somehow righted itself in the last twelve hours.

He nods slowly. "My boys. Billy and Sam. Say hello to, uh, Remy. Remember your manners."

I hear nothing else after he utters my name. His voice is as deep and growly as I remember it. As resonant. I shake Billy's hand—he's the climber, and let Sam off the hook with another smile, hopefully one that doesn't scare him this time.

My reward is a tiny grin. A slight rotation of his tiny body around Logan's massive thigh. His young gaze pings beyond me to the sack of copper pennies on the battered workbench. "Why is your money so shiny?"

That he recognises copper as money warms my heart. I beckon him forward and retrieve the bag of coins. "I polished these ones to make a countertop with. Any leftovers will be necklaces, but sometimes I make those with tarnished pennies too."

"Tarnished?"

"Like this." I fish my pendant from beneath my clothes and show Sam both sides of it. "I cleaned it up a bit when I made it, but that was a long time ago and I like it better now it shows its age."

"Like Dad and the beard he gets when he doesn't work for a whole week?"

A rumble of a laugh comes from behind me and it's a glorious sound. Logan joins us at the workbench. He musses Sam's hair with one hand and lifts the pendant from my palm with the other. "I remember this. Didn't get a good look at it, though."

"What were you looking at instead?" It's out of my mouth before I can stop it. No regrets, but he's with his kids. Flirting with a dude might be a hard limit. Then I see the heat flare in his luminous green eyes and that worry disappears.

He's pleased to see me.

Logan's said nothing to substantiate a claim that bold, but I feel it. See it in the way he leans closer to me with the warmest smile lighting his earnest face before he catches himself and lets the pendant fall.

It drops back to my chest. He watches it, then lifts his gaze to mine, holding me there, as if he knows I need a minute to fixate on his mouth. To *remember* his mouth and how it felt when he kissed me.

Kissed you back, you mean. You pounced on him first.

I think. That night was hazy for multiple reasons and a lot has happened since. All I know for sure is that his kiss was fucking magical.

"I was looking at your skin," Logan says. It feels sudden, but only because I'm distracted by everything about him. "In case you got burnt."

"Ah. Yeah. You were gonna save me. I remember now."

"Something like that." Logan's gaze flits to Sam as tiny hands reach for my sack of coins. "Oi. Don't touch."

"It's fine." I upend the sack onto the bench, letting the pennies fall wherever. "I have loads more."

Billy appears at the bench, eyes wide. "Are you rich?"

"Nah, I got them from a skip."

He doesn't believe me, I can tell. But he's fascinated by the coins, so I lift him onto the bench so he can see them better.

The movement strains the fragile bones in my shoulder. Billy doesn't weigh much, but it hurts enough that I swallow a grimace and clamp my arm to my side once I've set him down.

Logan hoists Sam onto the bench too. Four tiny hands delve into the coins and he sends me a sceptical glance. "You sure about this? They'll be covered in ketchup and Marmite before you know it."

"It's fine." In truth, if I'm going to meet the order deadlines hanging over me, I don't have time to clean the coins again. But I like watching kids play with old things. Gongs and drums. Bendy sticks and pine cones. It reminds me that life is simple when you want it to be.

Also, the longer Logan's boys mess with the coins, the longer he has to stand in the workshop I'm fairly certain belongs to his uncle. *The boy handles the money.*

Logan is all man, but there's no other explanation I can think of for his appearance at the top of Firefly Hill. There's nothing here but me.

We drift back from the boys. Logan glances around the workshop a few times, but eventually, his attention settles on me. He eyes the arm I'm holding tight to my ribs, perhaps seeing more than I want him to. But this version of him seems to be a quiet man—not that festival Logan was loud—and he keeps his thoughts to himself, his only question one that he could've plucked right out of my head. "How the hell are you here?"

The answer isn't one I want to give. Not when all I see when I look at him is everything I want to do to his thick, strong body. I back up to a stack of boxes and lean against it, taking the weight off my hip, just for a moment. "Might ask you the same thing. You're a long way from Leicestershire."

"It's not that far, and I live here. You sound *Welsh*."

"So? You can probably see the motherland from the top of this hill. If you discount the fact I haven't been there in more than a decade, I'm not that far from home."

"And your name is Remy?"

"Uh-huh. And you're Logan."

"I am." Logan rocks back on his heels. "My uncle is your landlord."

"I figured. You come to shake me down for the rent already?"

"You're clear till January."

"December."

Logan shakes his head. "Nope. Marr wanted you to get through Christmas first."

"Why?"

Billy picks up a penny and flicks it at his brother. Logan rumbles like an alpha wolf. It's...hot. And effective. The boys go back to ignoring us and comparing the dates on the coins.

Logan watches them a moment, then rotates his attention back to me. "He didn't explain himself. Never does. It's my job to make sure you don't trash the place and that you pay on time, whenever he's decided that is. If it's different to what you agreed, you'll have to take it up with him."

"I'm not about to complain about an extra month's grace. I'm just confused. He's not like any landlord I've ever come across before."

"You get used to it. Actually, you don't. But he's a good man. If you don't fuck him over, he'll be your pal for life."

I'm not going to complain about that either. The world away from the bright lights and crowded fields is a lonely one. If

Uncle Marr wants to be my mate, I can dig it. "What about you?"

Logan tilts his head. "What about me?"

"What does it take for you to be my friend?"

"You wanna be my friend, Remy?"

There it is—the fire we left in the wet grass, still burning bright. I felt it as soon as I saw him, but it's shed its winter skin and it's as potent as ever. I remember him striding across the arena to me. There's less space between us now, but he narrows it with as much determination.

Stops half a foot away from me, but he's close enough that his body heat hits me. *He runs hot*. I like it. It suits him and the sparks dancing in his electric gaze. He's a giant. An emotive one. Even if I wasn't half drunk on him already, I could stare at him all day long.

I clench my fists to stop from reaching for him. I'm not sure he'd push me away, but his kids are here, and when I touch him next, I'm not going to stop at a kiss.

A wild thought for a casual introduction, but I'm tired of being careful.

I'm *tired*, full stop. Maybe if I wasn't, rational thought would remind me I haven't answered any of his questions except to confirm my name.

Logan doesn't seem to have noticed. He stares at my mouth and I stare at his. It seems to be all we have until one of the boys calls for him.

I'm too wired to know which one. And I don't resent them stealing his attention. He's the same dad I saw at the park. Kind. Sweet. Fair. I watch him wrangle the boys into sweeping the coins back into their bag. Mediate the squabbling with a patience my parents never had.

It's as alluring as his muscled back and chiselled jaw, and keeps me in place instead of helping them. I don't get up until they're done.

I cross the workshop with Logan's gaze all over me. It's all of three strides, but the ache in my hip is here to stay until I get some dry heat into it, and it's hard to hide.

His stare turns curious. I ignore it and reach for the bag. I retrieve a handful of pennies and drop them into each boys' hand. "Swap them for your old ones and I'll show you how to polish them one day."

"You don't have to do that," Logan murmurs too soft for them to hear.

I ignore that too, because I'm having a sudden trouble looking at him, as if my brain doesn't want to confront the reality that he's about to leave. I know myself well enough to trust I'd have made the same invitation to anyone's children, but I can't deny their enthusiasm reassures me I'll see him again.

The boys say goodbye and scamper under the door.

Logan follows them until he reaches the hanging metal. I stay by the workbench, waiting for him to limbo his tall frame beneath it, but he lingers, his big hand resting on the corrugated steel. "I know this is weird as hell, but, um, can we talk again? One day, maybe?"

"Talk?"

"Yeah." He shifts from one foot to the other. "I'm shit at stuff like this so it's probably going to come out wrong, but I think about you a lot and I don't want the summer to end with me asking for my uncle's rent money."

Aside from the fact that summer ended for me the moment I fell off the back of a moving rig, every word out of his mouth is perfect, and the uncertainty in his sea-green eyes kills me.

There's a foot or so between us.

I close it and, slowly, reach for his other hand, giving him time to evade if he doesn't want his boys to see him touch another man.

Logan doesn't move. He lets me take his hand and slot our

fingers together, taking a breath as he feels the same tranquillity of the moment that I do.

That contradicting calm. A stillness that should be in conflict with the rushing current that sweeps through me, but somehow only adds to the feeling of *right* I've been chasing since we kissed all those months ago.

He doesn't kiss me this time.

I don't kiss him either. I want to, but I settle for squeezing his fingers instead.

He squeezes back, a beat of *I feel it too.*

Then he lets go with a reluctant sigh. "It's getting late. You probably want to get home. I'll come find you tomorrow, maybe?"

"I'll be here." Course I will. I have nowhere else to go and even before he brightened my day, I wasn't that sad about it. "Can't make you a cuppa, though. I haven't got a kettle."

A smile lights Logan's rugged face. "We'll figure it out."

Story of my life. I grin back as he finally stoops to duck back under the door.

I should let him go.

I *should*. But his name tumbles from my lips and he stops, bent over, his gaze hooked on mine. "Yeah?"

"It was good, right? The night we met?"

His fading smile returns. "Better than good."

I nod. "That's what I thought. I was off my tits on booms, but I've remembered it every day since as the best kiss I've ever had."

Logan laughs. "Me too. Without the booms. Take care, Remy. I'll see you soon."

His laughter, that warm, rich sound, keeps me company all night long.

I've slept alone in this bed every night since I bought it two years ago, but the absence of someone beside me, that silence, still rocks me every time I wake up.

Even when I'm not alone.

There's a sole of an elf-sized foot pressed to my cheek. *Billy.* Little shit. He doesn't sneak into my bed for affection. He wants to watch cartoons in the morning and he knows it's a good time of day to push his luck.

I've worked too many horrible night shifts to be a morning person. That moment when the sun rises and the world is still the same brutal place it was in the dark—it haunts me. I'd rather pull a pillow over my head and keep sleeping.

Preferably without the foot in my face.

It's not quite dawn yet. In fact, it's a long way off. A squint at my phone tells me it's 4 am.

I roll out of bed and scoop Billy up. The boys' bedroom is next to mine. I carry him in and set him on his top bunk. He doesn't stir, thank God. I love my boys, but I'm parented out, and even in this hazy state I have too much on my mind to deal with Billy and his occasional inability to sleep the whole night through without mischief.

When I'm sure he's settled, I creep away. I should go back to bed, but a compulsion drives me to the landing window and its unobscured view up Firefly Hill, a wide expanse of grass and trees, broken only by the dirt track and the plain concrete walls of my uncle's workshop.

Remy's workshop.

I love his name.

It's the one thought I have before the light beneath the rolling door registers in my sleepy mind.

Damn. He's there already. That's dedication. Last time I looked it was just after ten last night and Remy had still been hard at work, hunched over the workbench, doing something I couldn't see from this distance.

In truth, I could hardly see him, but I'd stared and stared and stared all the same.

I stare now too, but the door is all the way closed, just the strip of low light, and the smoke from the chimney, visible in the dark night.

"I haven't got a kettle."

A consuming urge sweeps over me to make that right. Not with a kettle—I don't have an Argos warehouse stashed under the bed—but with a mug of something hot. Despite the burner, that workshop is *cold.* But it's dick o'clock in the morning and we don't know each other, not really. Rocking up uninvited twice in twelve hours feels strange, even for a friendship that began with a kiss in the rain.

I force myself from the window and go back to bed. In the time it's taken me to creep on Remy and wrestle with the idea of an intrusive cup of tea, Sam has rolled from his bed and into mine.

He's less chaotic about it than his brother, curled up on the very edge, a fluffy turtle toy clutched to his chest. But cute as he is, fair is fair. I give him the same treatment as Billy, then slide back under the covers.

My kids have kept the bed warm, I'll give them that, and I run hot at the best of times, but as I flop against the pillows, the sheets feel cold. A shiver passes through me that has nothing to do with temperature and everything to do with the fact that I haven't had an adult conversation since the five minutes I spent with Remy yesterday.

Also, I can't stop thinking about holding his hand, his long fingers laced with mine. I imagine rubbing his knuckles with the pad of my thumb, tracing the chakra tattoos. Before yesterday, I'd imagined his hands as delicate things, but up close, without the magic of a festival night around us, his hands were scarred and hardened by work. And as ethereal as his smile still is, there isn't anything *delicate* about him.

He's all man.

I like that thought. My sexuality is undefined enough that I can go either way with most things, but I like the scruff on Remy's face, the masculine set of his jaw, and the deep timbre of his voice. It makes my stomach flutter and my cock pulse, and he's not even here.

Holy hell. I roll onto my belly, flattening my arousal to the mattress. I'm not above rubbing one out to my mythical friend who now has a name, but my bedroom door is open and my boys are home. Wanking over the dude up the hill will have to wait.

I don't get any more sleep, but the morning seems to rush up on me anyway. It's a mess of spilt Coco Pops, burnt toast, and stubbing my fucking toe on the box of Christmas decorations I dragged from the loft last night.

It's too early for tinsel and baubles, but I've learnt the hard way to go all in when I have the time, in case I don't when it matters. Stockings, tree presents, dinner, I missed it all last year. Never made it home, and I don't know if Bec's gonna grant me a do-over.

I take the kids to school via the park. Sam is still scared of heights and I want to fix that by summer. Slow progress, but all the best things are, right?

Like sex. The thought barrels into me as I'm driving home. I try to shake it off, but it's tenacious and my body heats, despite the cracked-open window blasting me with arctic chill.

My mind drifts to Remy. I've imagined fucking him more times than I care to admit, but that was way back in that other life when I honestly thought I'd never see him again. Sixteen hours since that changed and it's like living those weeks after Greenfest on repeat, only this time in ultra-high definition.

I shift in my seat, trying to ignore the tightness in my jeans. They're old enough that they should give me a bit of room, but Remy, man. He does something to me I can't explain. Like a Christmas present that sits under the tree from the beginning of December, glittering in the dark.

Right, because you're going to unwrap him?

Jesus Christ, I'm a daft twat.

I rub my face, trying to get my head in the game, but without the boys or work to distract me, he's all I see. I can't stop thinking about him, naked or otherwise.

Focus on the otherwise. He said you could talk again. No one said anything about fucking.

As if him holding my hand isn't the most erotic thing that's ever happened to me.

God, this would be easier if he hadn't echoed my thoughts seconds before I walked away from him. *"...best kiss I've ever had."*

Can't argue with that. Before him, kissing wasn't my thing. Still isn't. I get laid on Scruff. Swing by a Premier Inn in the city for pump and dumps that make me feel like shit. I treat people well and I *know* I make them feel good, but it's mechanical. An emptiness I've convinced myself is all I have time for. All I *want*. But that feeling, man, that energy Remy left me with last summer...

I crave it.

Firefly Hill looms in the distance. I drive to the foot of it and follow the icy, winding road on autopilot, parking outside my house. The whole way, I win the battle not to fixate on the workshop above, but the moment I'm out of the car, I'm done.

I slam the door and rotate to face the ascending dirt track, and because lightning really does strike twice—three times, whatever—the object of my blood-heating desire is right in front of me.

He's an angel, I swear. The winter sun is behind him, making his hair shine, and his shadow catches mine before the reality that he's a solid person, not a figment of my overactive imagination, hits home.

His boots crunch on the frosty ground. He reaches the end of my drive and I'm there waiting for him, the fact that I have a million things to do today so far from my mind I forget all about it.

I forget everything except his dazzling half grin. "Morning."

Remy stops at my broken gate. It's been open and hanging off since Bec drove into it six months ago. "Morning. You all right?"

It's a greeting, not an enquiry about my general state, and for that, I'm glad. What would I say? Tired with a mix of rabidly horny?

I nod in lieu of answering, then frown as I realise he has a bag on his back, his jacket buttoned up to his chin, and boots on his feet that aren't suitable for a damp hike. "Where you off to?"

"Town." Remy inclines his head down the hill. "I need some stuff from the hardware shop on the high street."

"Van got no diesel?"

I'm joking, but Remy pulls a face that tells me I'm right on the money. "I forgot."

Something feels off, but I let it go, hyper-focused on how cold it is instead, and the fact that he clearly has an injury that isn't going to thank him for a three mile round trip with hills and steep steps. "Screwfix delivers as far as my place. Get them to bring it to you."

"Nah." Remy rolls his shoulders with a subtle wince. "I've only got cash and I'd rather give it to a shop that's been there a hundred years than some faceless corporation."

He means it, I can tell, and leans away, gearing up to move off. I need to be in my house, cleaning something, washing something, picking junk up before I trip over and die—it happens, I've seen it. But the idea of Remy tramping in the cold and the wind when I have a vehicle with a full tank of fuel just hits wrong.

Nope.

Not doing it. "Take my car."

Remy's fair brows arch. "Huh? Oh, no. You're all right. I can't do that."

"Why not?"

"Um..." For the first time, Remy's the one who trips over his words. "I don't have insurance right now. It ran out a few days ago, so no driving for me until I renew the policy on the van."

No fuel. No insurance. Put together with Uncle Marr's port-in-a-storm rent agreement and I'm starting to build a picture that makes my grumpy heart pinch. Something's up, and not in the good way. I want to help, but I remember being on my arse and the few friends I have trying to help *me*.

How it felt.

How much I fucking *hated* it. "Okay. How about this? It's early Friday, I need to pick the boys up at lunchtime today. I can give you a lift then if you can wait that long?"

Remy's gaze turns shrewd, seeing right through me, but the wind chooses that moment to pick up, whistling up the hill with a brutal zip.

It rattles him. He cringes against it and sighs. "All right."

"Come by just before twelve?"

"Works for me." His smile is quiet this time. He sets off up the dirt track and I watch him move, eyeing the leg that moves just a beat too slow. I'm no doctor, but it looks like his left hip is fucking his mobility. It's subtle, but combined with the pain I saw in his face when he lifted Billy, I'm wondering what the hell has happened in the months since I last saw him.

I wonder so hard that I'm still standing there when he reaches the workshop and glances down.

Damnit.

I wheel around and stride to my front door, but the damage is done. He caught me staring and I don't even care.

The next few hours pass like the minute hand is stuck on the grandfather clock in my hallway. I wash PE kits and bedsheets. Fix the broken dishwasher and take a shower with a boner I somehow manage to ignore.

I watch the time like my life depends on it, but somehow the soft knock at the front door still makes me jump. *You're not used to visitors.*

Yup. That's definitely it.

I pad through the house in socked feet and open the door.

Remy leans against the porch, a half-smile curving his mouth. He looks the same as he did three hours ago, but I hone in on different details this time: his lush lips, the wave in his blond hair. The fact that his eyes are so warm I could happily drown in them. "Hey, Papa."

I grin. "Something wrong with my name?"

"Papa suits you better. You're like a big bear."

"I've changed my mind. You can hoof it into town after all."

I back up to let him know I'm joking and wave him inside.

44

Remy hesitates a moment, then steps over the threshold.

I reach over him and shove the door shut. He's not short—five-eleven, something like that. But he's right about me being *big*. I have six inches on him and our close proximity forces him to look up at me.

His eyes are bottomless. I sink into his gaze by mistake. It catches me unawares, snaring me. The door closes with a clunk, but I remain all up in his face, and I can't seem to make myself move.

Remy's smile widens a touch. "It's still there, isn't it?"

"Don't know what you mean," I deadpan.

"Liar."

It's a strange thing that he feels so familiar to me. Maybe it's because I've replayed that kiss in my head a thousand times since the summer. But it's not just the zippy current that wraps around me like an old friend. It's his scent and his droll amusement. His quiet footsteps as I finally give him the space to venture further into my house.

My *cottage*. It's way too small to call anything else. Just a hallway, a kitchen and a lounge downstairs. Two bedrooms and a bathroom on the second floor. There's a loft I've got grand plans to convert, but who the hell knows if I'll ever do it.

"That's the problem, Lo. Everything you want to do takes a thousand years."

Dear Lord. I'm not in the mood to hear my ex berating me in my head. I try to tune her out, but as Remy glances around the mess and chaos only living with boys can bring, I find myself nervous.

I scratch my jaw, scraping my fingers through the scruff that grows back by five o'clock every day I don't have to shave it for work.

"Who's that?"

"Hmm?"

Remy has paused by the little table at the end of the hall. It's

MDF and ugly as shit, but there's nowhere else to keep the old framed photographs I rescued from the house I shared with Bec.

"My brother."

"You look scarily alike, apart from the hair."

"We're twins."

"Oh." Remy peers closer at the picture. It's five years old and shows my brother with Billy and Sam perched on each shoulder. "He dyes his hair?"

"Nope. Came out like that. We're fraternal twins, but identical in every other physical way."

"He's hot."

"So he tells me every time I see him."

Remy spins to face me. "He's not as hot as you, Papa."

"Thanks." I prop a shoulder on the nearest wall. "You want a tea or something?"

"Or something?" Remy's grin amps up *another* notch. "What does that entail?"

He's winding me up. For once I'm glad my brother stayed in Devon to fuck his life up there, while I followed Bec wherever she told me to. I don't need two men in my life who can run rings around me.

Also, the thread Remy's tugging on is volatile. I've never been as drawn to someone as I am to him. I don't know where it ends. So I speak the truth, like I always do, a strength or a weakness, depending who you ask. "It entails everything I don't have time for. I have to pick the boys up soon."

"Probably just as well. I'm fascinated by you. But I don't have a lot of time right now either."

It feels like the end of something that hasn't begun. I want it to shift back, but the world doesn't work that way. Things happen or they don't.

I find my boots and stamp into them. By the time I'm done, Remy has drifted back to the front door.

He's poking at a box of festive ornaments. "Getting started early?"

I dig my keys from the bowl of junk by the door. "Trying to. Work is crazy over Christmas. Don't know if I'll be here when it matters."

There's a gloom in my voice I didn't authorise. I walk away from it, opening the front door to the harsh wind and stepping outside.

Remy follows me.

The door shuts behind him. It locks, but I check anyway, leaning over him again, absolutely not tracking his tongue as he drags it over his bottom lip. "You're a firefighter? At the station in town?"

I shake my head. "In the city. Blue Watch."

"Does that mean your hat is blue?"

"It's a helmet. And no. It's yellow, like everyone else's. Blue means the shift crew I'm on."

I head for the car, sensing Remy at my back as he trails after me.

The Discovery is too crap for central locking. I unlock the driver door, climb inside, and click the other side. Remy slides into the passenger seat and wedges his bag at his feet. It could go in the boot, but I don't want to micromanage him. That he's in my car at all seems a fragile universe.

My car is full of junk. Toys, crisp packets, empty Fruit Shoot bottles. I feel the same way about it that I did in the house, but Remy doesn't notice the carnage. He reaches for the CDs wedged in the door and flips through them, gaze narrowed in concentration, and I take my cue to start the engine.

The cold doesn't bother me, but Remy's two stone behind me and he's wearing a denim jacket. I flip the heaters on and subtly point them in his direction while he's engrossed in my questionable music taste.

My reward comes from his pursed lips as he restrains his

laughter. "Slipknot, Ocean Colour Scene, *and* Cher? Dude, that's quite a mix."

"Hey, at least it's not boring," I defend. "And the metal is my brother's."

"Interesting that it's Slipknot you're distancing yourself from and not Cher's *Greatest Hits* album."

"Give a shit. I love Cher."

Remy does laugh this time and it's so melodic and gorgeous I have trouble focussing on the road. "You're right," he says when he calms down. "You're never boring, Papa."

It confounds me that I like that nickname. That he even has one for me when we've been reacquainted such a short time. But I do like it. As long as he doesn't call me it when we're—

My brain screeches to a halt. When we're what? Fucking in the shower? Rolling around a bed that's only seen my goddamn hand? What the hell is wrong with me? We left the house with some unspoken boundaries and I'm already kicking them down.

A cool hand skates over my forearm.

Remy's hand. I blink and look at him.

He gnaws on his bottom lip. "I'm sorry. Did I annoy you already?"

"Huh?"

"Your face folded into a thousand knots." He starts to reach for me with his other hand, then seems to catch himself and his touch slides away. "I ramble when I'm nervous. I wasn't taking the piss, I swear."

I make an attempt to un-pickle my face. "I know you weren't. It's okay. Why are you nervous around me?"

Remy averts his gaze and I have to divert mine back to the road. A beat of silence fills the car, and the Discovery chooses that moment to play its party trick, blasting out music no-one asked it for.

It's the Christmas radio station and Carol of the Bells, from *Home Alone*, ambushes us, the volume almost fucking violent.

I fumble for the knob to turn it down.

Remy's hand is already there and our fingers tangle, a mess of chemistry and awkwardness before he wrenches his hand away. "That's why. Something happens to me when I'm around you. It's weird, right? This thing?"

I swivel the knob on the radio, playing for time. It would be easier to deny it. To let him think it was all in his head so I wouldn't have to confront the fact that I'm obsessed with someone I barely know. That I don't have the time or emotional energy to think about him as much as I am.

But I can't deny it.

I don't want to. "It *is* weird. I told my brother about you a while ago—about what happened at Greenfest and how I couldn't stop thinking about it. About *you*. He reckons we knew each other in a past life, but he also likes Slipknot and puts milk in green tea, so..."

Remy laughs again, but it's not as joyous this time. It's bemused. Uncertain. Almost sad.

I don't want him to feel like that, about me or anything else. I steer the car onto the main road, wishing we were somewhere else so I could give him my full attention.

Home Alone gives way to Please Come Home for Christmas. The Charles Brown song is maudlin beneath the soft blues beats, but it's my brother's favourite, so I leave it on.

Remy falls quiet and gazes out the window. His eyes seem heavy. I let him be, wondering if he'll doze off, but he's awake when we reach town a little while later.

I pull onto the high street and stop in the taxi rank, ignoring the signs and the irate drivers who know I'm not a motherfucking cab.

Remy is lost in thought. I consider touching him. *Burn* for it, but he comes to before I can kick that can of worms.

49

"Fuck. Sorry. World of my own."

"Is it a good one?"

The sadness returns. "Used to be. Thanks for the lift, Papa. I'll see you around."

He wraps a hand around the door handle, preparing to leave. Something catches in my chest and I feel unreasonably compelled to stop him. "Can I give you a ride back up the hill too?"

Remy tilts his head and gives me this *look*. Half defeated and half amused, I can't explain it. "I'll be okay."

"Sure about that? It's a long way in the cold, I've done it drunk enough times."

"Really? You don't seem the type."

"To get arseholed and stumble home? Fucking hell, who do you think I am?"

"A man with responsibilities."

That, I can't deny. But the first part of that sentence is what matters. "I'm just a man, Remy. I make a mess of myself as much as the next dude."

Finally, he smiles again. "You're not just a man, Logan. If you were, I'd have forgotten all about you."

He exits the car before I can answer. I'm not ready to admit how long I sit there, watching him walk away.

Remy

This necklace is where it all began. Braided leather. An old penny, shaped and hung. I've made too many variations to remember each one, but this one, just the penny and the leather, reminds me where I came from.

On days like today, it should remind me that I've landed on my arse for the time being, but the work is so familiar I can't find the despair I've lived with for months and months now.

I shove an extra log on the stove without worrying when I'll have the money to buy more. With my new files and drill bits, I make twelve copper pendants and set them aside to wrap later when the night draws in and I need something to do.

Then I spend an hour on the copper tabletop. It's heavy, but sleeping in the dry workshop has done me the world of good. I move it around like the old me, and I feel good.

I feel even better when my Etsy app pings with new orders, most of them simple enough, but there's a ring enquiry that catches my attention.

Two men's rings.

Get in. Rings are fiddly and they take time I don't have. But the mark up on wedding bands is worth the hours I'll spend at my workbench getting them done.

Done with the table, I search for the bag that contains the coins from the rest of the world. The bag is my most valuable possession outside of my tools and hunk of junk van, but somehow I've lost track of it.

It's nowhere in the workshop. *The van.* Fuck's sake. It's mid-afternoon, but I'm pretty much shut up for the night, door down all the way now I've fixed the mechanism, stove lit, trying to keep the place warm for the long night ahead. But if I don't check the van tonight, it'll bug me every second till I fall asleep on the mattress I dragged inside yesterday.

Sighing, I crank the door and duck outside to the van. Still without diesel. Still uninsured.

But I'm getting there. The tabletop is almost finished. Once it's gone, I can dip into the money I took for it and get my life together. Insure the van. Buy some food that isn't dehydrated. I'm a long way off being able to rent an actual place to live, but by the summer it won't matter.

Then what? You'll do this every winter?

Long-term thinking is new to me. Before this summer, I thought I was invincible.

Then again, before *Logan*, little old me thought a kiss was just a kiss.

I turn the inside of the van upside down and discover the magic bag stuffed under the front seat. The coins are cold and it's dark, but I dump it on the seat and sift through them anyway, not sure what I'm looking for until I find the old Spanish pesetas and Hungarian forints.

The Spanish coins are a faded gold with centre holes already in place, and I only have three of them. *Don't fuck it up.*

Heh. I like a challenge. Preferably one that doesn't hinge on surviving the night.

I pocket the coins I need and stuff the bag back under the seat. The van door needs slamming twice to close properly. On my second go, I hear the rumble of a vehicle below, then the unmistakable shouts of siblings as they get out of a car mid-argument.

Logan's kids. I'm already smiling before I glance down Firefly Hill. I haven't seen him since he gave me a lift into town last week, and I haven't seen his boys since the hottie from the park turned out to be my summer fantasy come true.

I never asked him about their mum. Didn't need to. Logan has divorced dad written all over every aspect of his life I've been lucky enough to see. I'm guessing he shares custody with his ex and the four days of silence from down the hill have coincided with him working.

He's a firefighter. Still makes me shiver, though it explains his strict dedication to fire marshalling duty at Greenfest.

"You had sparks all over you."

Inside me, actually, the second I caught him watching me.

Ho hum.

Logan is last out of the car. He unfolds his tall frame from behind the wheel and scrubs a hand through his dark hair before intervening in the boys' fight. From here, I can't see every detail in his handsome face, but his weary amusement is hard to miss, and it looks good on him.

The amusement, at least. Thinking of Logan in any way that isn't happy contentment—*or naked*—makes my stomach flip and I'm too hungry right now to cope with that.

I don't have to stay hungry, though. The ring order has been paid upfront. I don't like spending money I haven't earned yet, but the thought of a hot meal in town is tempting enough that I consider braving the walk. Maybe something spicy to shift the tightness I still feel in my chest.

Daydreaming about dragon chicken helps me pull away from the domestic perfection below me. I take my coins inside and fiddle with them until the noise in my belly is too loud to ignore.

Outside, sleet is falling. It's almost snow, but not quite. Too wet. No lie, it's basically rain on steroids. But I'm hungry, and I'm sick of noodles and packet rice.

I shrug on my coat and find a hat to squish down my hair. I washed it in the sink last night and it's been having a party on my head ever since.

The black beanie is warm from being near the stove. It's a hug for my skull and makes me feel more like a nap than a hike, but dinner, man. I'm excited.

I lock up and leave, almost forgetting that my downhill adventure will take me past Logan's broken gate.

Then I hear the boys shouting again, but with laughter this time instead of childhood rage. I draw closer and see them running around the driveway, pelting each other with wet slush. It's cute and carefree, and the mud splashed up their clothes is another clue that if their mum is anything like mine, she's nowhere within a ten-mile radius right now.

Logan is, though. He's leaning in the doorway, mug in one hand, his shoulder propped on the frame.

He doesn't see me right away. His eyes have that fatigued haze that doesn't see much at all.

The boys spot me first. Billy skids to a stop in front of me. "You're the penny man."

"Penny Remy, that's me."

"I put my shiny coins in my money box. Dad made me take some out, though. They're on the fireplace with Sam's."

"That's good. We can polish them next time you come up to the shop."

"Can we do it now?"

"Not today, old chap. I'm off for my dinner."

Billy frowns and peers down the hill. "Where are you going?"

"Town. Gonna find me something spicy."

"But it's wet."

"So are you."

Billy accepts my counterargument. If it had just been me and him, I might've been home free. Or not home, depending on how you look at it. But Sam spies me next and Billy tells him my grand plan.

Sam's shaking his head before Billy's even finished. "You can't walk down Firefly Hill in the rain. It's the rules."

"It's not raining. Look." I hold out my hand and let sleet fall on my palm. "You can't catch raindrops."

"It's still too wet. And it's nighttime. Dad says the cars can't see you in the dark and all your clothes are black."

"My trousers are blue. And what cars are going to come up if your dad's already here?"

It's a true story that only Logan and the postman drive up Firefly Hill. In the week that I've been here, I haven't seen another soul.

Sam doesn't care. "Why do you need to go down there? Dad says you went shopping already."

"That was last week."

"He's going for his tea," Billy says distantly, already bored with this ridiculous and sweet negotiation. "Which is stupid because he can just have tea here."

Of course those words leave his mouth as Logan steps off the porch and strides down the driveway, his long legs giving me no reprieve.

He's on us in seconds. "It's not the worst idea I've ever heard."

I can barely face him, he's so goddamn hot. "No? What is?"

"Whatever led up to that statement. Going for a walk?"

"Man's gotta eat."

"Man's gotta keep warm too. If you don't want to stay, at least let us drive you into town."

Absolutely not. The fact that I can't drive myself is my problem, not his. Also, I'm not taking him away from his cosy home when he looks as tired as he does right now. "I've got legs for a reason. I'll be fine."

Logan shrugs as if he's letting it go, but his kids are more tenacious. Billy climbs up the broken gate so we're eye level.

"It's still stupid. Dad made sausages and he always cooks too many. Why don't you just eat them?"

I want to make a sausage joke, but I'm not sure Logan will appreciate it in front of his young kids. I ponder blagging that I'm a vegetarian, but when they catch me later with bacon, we're all in trouble. "Um..."

"Hey." Logan pitches his voice lower than most kids pay attention too. Case-in-point, Billy is already slithering down the gate. "No pressure, but there's plenty of food and it's nice to have another adult at the table."

"You want my company, Papa?"

"Course I do. You know how many times I've discussed who burps the loudest at the dinner table this past month? If you won't save yourself, at least save me."

He walks away.

Sam waits and this kid's eyes are fucking *huge*. Like, massive balls of sea-glass persuasion. I'm still craving that spicy chicken, but damn, I crave these people more.

"All right." I slip through the broken gate and hold out my hand to Sam. "No burping, though, okay? You'll blow me away with those big lungs of yours."

Sam giggles and takes my hand, tugging me to the house. It might've felt weirder if I hadn't been inside before, but the hallway is familiar enough that I don't feel out of place.

We take our shoes off and Sam instantly disappears. I follow the sound of computer games to the living room and discover both boys already engrossed.

"Won't hear a fucking thing till there's food on the table."

I spin around. Logan is behind me. He grins a little, relieves me of my coat and hat, then jerks his head, signalling for me to follow him.

When I've ditched my boots, he leads me to the kitchen. It's a small, warm space with a round wooden table and scratched worktops. The appliances are old and basic, but the smell coming from the oven sways me on my feet.

Real food. I don't care what it is, I just want to eat it. "Can I help you with anything?"

Logan's gaze sweeps me, making more of the question than I meant. But he only shakes his head. "Sit down. Wanna beer?"

"Sure."

He brings bottles of cold Stella to the table and sits in the seat beside me. It's too close and nowhere near close enough, and I'm not inclined to analyse that. I'm attracted to him. It's hardly news. But I'm not set up for a casual bang on the kitchen table, and neither is he.

"Thanks for the invite," I say when he doesn't speak. "I mean, it's more of a hostage situation, but if whatever you're cooking ends up in my belly, I'm not complaining."

Logan tips beer down his throat, then licks his lips. "It's not that exciting, there's just a lot of it. Leftovers are life when I'm knackered from night shifts."

That explains the shadows beneath his eyes and the scratch in his voice. "How many did you do?"

"Just two, but last night"—he breaks off to yawn— "overran. Didn't get home till lunchtime."

"Did you sleep?"

"Nah. The boys finish school at three. No fucking point."

I'm tired too, but my reasons seem trivial next to his, and the fact that *he's* cooking *me* dinner feels back to front.

Fix it. But I can't. Logan's not a man who'd let someone kick him out of his kitchen, and honestly? I'm not much of a cook.

I can wash up, though. Pack leftovers and get him another

beer. It means not scarfing my dinner and running—literally—for the hill, but I can live with that. Logan's house is a nice place to be. It's messy and lived in and perfect.

Logan's a quiet man. He doesn't say much as we sit together, drinking beer. He asks about my work. I ask about his as much as I can without dragging whatever kept him on shift into the open.

He watches me a lot, though. As if I puzzle him. I figure out what it is when I spot the same box of decorations I saw the other day has migrated to the kitchen.

I get up to look and I've been sitting long enough that my shoulder reminds me that it's the tyrannical fun police. I limp a bit too, just once, but I return with the box to his deep, *deep* frown.

"Did something happen to you?"

"Hmm?"

"Since the summer. You're moving like you've been in a car crash."

His bluntness seems to surprise even him. He cringes. "Sorry. I could've put that better."

"It's okay. You're not far off." I open the box of decorations and fish out some knotted tinsel. "I fell off the back of a rig."

"Where?"

"A festival down south."

"How?"

My fingers move of their own accord to unpick the glittery strands I've dumped on the table. "Some dickheads stole a tractor from the hosting farm. They rammed the rig I was working on and the impact knocked me down."

Logan spins his empty bottle on the scarred table. "What did you break?"

"This side of me." I gesture to my shoulder and down my body. "Snapped collarbone, dislocated shoulder, fractured hip."

Logan cringes for real this time. "Did you hit your head?"

"No, thankfully. It hasn't felt right since, though."

He nods, understanding—*empathy*—filling his gaze without the pity that makes me a contrary arsehole. "You were off your feet a while then?"

Still am. I hum instead of giving voice to the truth, and I'm saved by the stove timer.

Logan gets up and pulls a tray of fat sausages from the oven. He sets them on the side and comes back to me, his seat sliding closer as he settles down.

By accident or design, I can't tell, but I'm more than okay with it. He smells good. He's warm. I lean into him without much conscious thought.

"I'm sorry that happened to you," he says quietly. "That night, watching you dance with the poi, I knew it was part of you. Losing it for a while must've hurt as much as the rest of it."

"It wasn't fun." I shoot him a dry smile that he returns. I track his lips as they rise and something stirs in me—something I might've been daft enough to indulge if Billy didn't burst into the kitchen.

I expect Logan to jump back.

He doesn't. His gaze lingers on me long enough for me to know he's still *right here* before he gives Billy his attention.

Billy runs into his arms. Logan scoops him up and dumps him in his lap. "No running in the kitchen. What you after, eh? Hungry?"

"I'm always hungry," Billy complains, then he zeroes in on the tinsel in my hands. "What are you doing?"

I show him. "Untangling it. I'm good with knots. Comes with the job."

"How?" Billy's brow furrows. "Pennies can't have knots."

"Leather does. Tiny necklace chains too."

"Oh." His frown remains.

Logan smooths it out with gentle fingers and tickles his son.

It's a pure kind of love I've never had. I absorb it, letting it warm my heart. This house, man. I didn't want to come in.

Now I don't want to leave.

Billy gets down and disappears again. Logan gets up to mash potatoes and open tins of baked beans.

Sam pops up behind me. "What are you doing?"

I explain it again. Sam drags a chair pretty much into my lap and sets about "helping".

To be fair, he's not half bad. I relinquish the tinsel and tackle the fairy lights instead. They're more of a jumble, and I sink into the work, answering Sam's random questions when they pop up.

I've half forgotten about dinner when Logan slaps it on the table.

"Wow. You weren't messing when you said there'd be a lot, eh?"

Logan shrugs. "Reasons still stand. Here..."

He slides me a plate and cutlery, then he whistles and Billy comes screeching back in.

They take their seats. I set the decorations aside and consider the mountain of sausages, mashed potatoes, and baked beans. There's gravy too, ketchup, HP, and...cranberry sauce?

"Sam's hooked on it," Logan answers my confusion. "Christmas all year round in this house."

"That's not a bad thing, surely?"

"I guess not." Logan edges the sausages towards me, the potatoes to Billy, and the beans to Sam.

He's too polite.

I'm about to tell him so when he gets up again and retrieves a bottle of hot sauce from the fridge.

"My addiction," he confesses. "Many a bad station dinner been saved by this magic."

"You're my fucking hero. Oops, sorry."

"For what? You think my kids don't hear an F-bomb every

six seconds on my watch?" Logan laughs at himself and points to the food. "Eat. It's all I need from anyone right now."

He doesn't have to tell his boys twice. They dive in, piling their plates high, and the amount of food Logan's cooked begins to make sense.

I almost feel bad taking any for myself, but I'm too hungry to be that emotional.

Silence descends as we eat. It's simple food, but damn, it's good. I eat and eat and eat until I sit back in my chair with a sigh.

Logan's done eating too. His gaze is shrewd. "Sure you've had enough? There's still loads left."

"I'm good."

"That's not what I asked."

"So?"

"All right." He nudges my leg under the table and harasses the boys instead, making them wipe their faces and clear up the mess around them.

They take the dishes to the counter.

Logan makes tracks to follow them, but I move first.

"Stay." I push him back into his seat. "I'm a shit cook, but I'd make a banging pot wash."

Logan's brows jump. Clearly, he's not used to being pushed and ordered around in his own home.

Oh well. I let my hand linger on his shoulder a moment. He's wearing a T-shirt so faded the red is this soft, vintage rust colour that makes his eyes greener than ever. The collar is loose and my fingers graze his throat, more than once.

"Relax," I murmur. "The bugs can help me if I put everything in the wrong place."

"They, uh," Logan breaks off as my fingertips ghost across his bare skin again. He sucks in a near silent, shaky breath and tries again. "They wouldn't care if you chucked it all out the back door."

"I won't do that."

"No?"

"*No.*" I bend down, lips a millimetre from his ear. He smells of smoke. It reminds me he's had a long night and day to get to this point. That getting him to stay where he is matters more than the simmering current between us.

I kiss him anyway, just once, on his rugged cheek, and whisper, "I promise."

The boys join me at the sink. We make messy work of washing up, but it gets done, and then comes the time where I should leave.

Logan presses another beer into my hand. "Stay. Please?"

He means for Netflix and chill. He points at the couch while mediating a squabble over Marvel movies.

The Incredible Hulk wins. I've never seen it, but the big green man is familiar enough that I sink into the sofa while Billy and Sam fetch snacks that land mainly on the rug ten minutes into the film.

They sit on beanbags on the floor.

Logan joins me on the couch.

"Dad," Billy calls, "who'd win if you had a fight with the Hulk?"

"Me."

"What about Uncle Locke? You're exactly the same."

"Locke's nicer, so still me." Logan stretches his long legs out. He's wearing grey joggers and it hits different than the jeans I've seen him in before.

"Locke's your hot twin?"

"Yeah."

"You're close?"

"Try to be. He's still in Devon, though, so we don't see him as much as we want to."

The west country lilt in his deep voice now makes sense. "You're a long way from home."

He shrugs. "So are you."

"I don't sound that Welsh. Not anymore."

"Keep telling yourself that, bro."

He grins into his beer and it's arresting enough that I don't argue. The film plays on and his couch is the most comfortable place I've been in months. My eyes grow lazy, but I fight them. I didn't come here to sleep through Logan's company.

Life's too short for that.

I sit up a little and set my empty beer bottle aside. Beside me, Logan's quiet, gaze flicking between the TV and his boys curled up at his feet.

His lids are heavy, eyes half closed. I take his beer bottle too and he barely notices.

Ten minutes tops.

It's less than that. The next time I glance sideways he's slipped lower and his arm is pillowing his head.

He's fast asleep and it's entrancing as hell.

You should leave.

Yup.

I turn the volume down on the TV and catch Sam's eye.

He's his father's son. Doesn't need telling a thing. He gets up and scampers off for a blanket. Comes back and lays it over his dad's legs.

Then he climbs onto the couch and passes out tucked against Logan's side.

Billy stays awake. He slips another film on and I let it happen. It feels intrusive to stay, but wrong to leave while Logan's sleeping, and there's no way in hell I'm waking him up.

Me and Billy are halfway through *Hawkeye* when he stirs.

"Shit." He heaves himself upright. "Sorry."

"You're all right." I hold out a hand to help him.

He blinks. Then takes it, wrapping his warm fingers around mine. "Is that *Hawkeye*?"

"Think so. Unless Billy put something else on." Straight up

not admitting I've spent the last hour watching him instead. That I'm hypnotised by his sleep-mussed hair and adorable bemusement.

Logan rubs his face, noticing Sam asleep beside him and the popcorn all over the carpet. "Fuck, we're a mess."

"Only the good kind." We're still holding hands. I reluctantly let go and force myself upright. "Thanks for dinner."

Still half asleep, Logan nods.

I knock fists with Billy and leave them to it.

I'm at the door when Logan calls my name.

For a big man, he's fast and light on his feet, behind me by the time I spin around.

I have my hand on his front door.

He takes it off and tucks it in both of his, like he's protecting it from evil. "I, uh. I just wanted to say thanks."

"What for?"

"The company. I love my kids. But sometimes I need something else when I come off a rough shift, you know?"

"What do you usually do?"

Logan's lips twitch. "That's a conversation for another day. If you ever wanna come back to this mad house."

I don't know if he realises, but he's got me pressed against the door. Beyond him, the hallway is dark. The boys are nowhere to be seen and something wicked-sweet unfurls inside me. "Your house is a nice place to be."

"Yeah?"

"Yeah." I love that I have to stretch up to kiss him. That a light brush of lips is a whole body experience.

I love that he's not as surprised this time as he was in that field under the stars.

Logan smiles into the kiss and cups my face with his big hand. He kisses me back with a gentle sweep of his tongue before he breaks away and lays his forehead against mine. "You're going to get me in trouble."

"How so?"

"I've been dreaming about doing that for half a fucking year. Now I've done it I'm gonna need a new hobby."

My hands find his hips, fingers wrapping over the soft waistband of his joggers, thumbs searching out the bare, scorching skin above.

He shivers at my touch, a light ripple that rattles his solid frame. It's so hot I forget whatever I was going to say. I have nothing except how it feels to have him this close again.

His simmering gaze and soothing body heat.

The charged buzz everywhere we touch.

I try not to think about how hard I am.

How hard he is—and how big. I still can't see or hear his kids, but they're out there somewhere. Young eyes, little ears. A whole world that isn't me and Logan welded together at his front door.

A *cold* world I have to step into the moment he lets me go.

If he lets me go. Right now, he's staring at me as if he's drowning and he's perfectly okay with that.

But I can't let him drown. Not tonight.

I let my thumbs skim the firm muscle beneath his faded tee one more time, then drop my hands. "I should go."

It breaks the spell. Logan blinks. Nods and steps back. "You'll be okay?"

"I'm not going to get lost between here and the workshop."

It's not what he meant, and I know it. But I'm not in the mood to confront the fact that he sees so much more than I'm prepared for.

I mourn the last of his warmth and reach behind me to open the door. "Goodnight, Papa."

Logan

I have four days off after Remy comes to dinner and we kiss in my dark hallway. You'd think I'd find plenty of opportunity to track him down for round two—or is it three by now?—but, no. When I'm working, I have zero energy for anything else.

So when I'm not, I spend most of my time playing catch-up. Food shopping, washing, paying the bills. Even my piece of shit car takes a slice of me with its overdue need for a service.

A service that costs me six hundred quid thanks to a water pump. I'm still stewing over that by the time the weekend rolls around and I'm swamped by swimming lessons, football clubs, and birthday parties. I swear to God, Bec only signs up for the ones that fall on my days.

I'm recovering from a zorbing screamfest when I finally catch sight of Remy. It sucks donkey balls that it's the crack of dawn and I'm on my way to work.

He doesn't see me. He's carrying a jerry can up the hill. Presumably, it's full of diesel for his van and I want to stop and tell him the dangers of fuel vapours as much as I want to do *so many other things* to him. But I don't have time. I need to deliver the boys to Bec and drive into the city for my shift.

Eight-till-six. A lot can happen in ten hours. Sometimes it's worse when it doesn't. The hours drag and with Remy on my mind, there's nowhere to hide.

Galen, my wingman on Blue Watch, sniffs out my wandering thoughts like a fucking bloodhound.

We're decorating the station Christmas tree. Current status: looks like an eighties branch of Woolworths threw up on it.

He hands me another length of pink tinsel. "All right. What's her name?"

"Whose name?"

"Whoever's got you staring into space and messing with your hair the way you used to when Bec had you in a spin."

I wind tinsel around the already overloaded tree. "Bec hasn't had me in a spin in years, least not the good kind. And stop obsessing over my hair. You wanna run your grubby fingers through it, go right ahead."

Galen catches the kiss I blow his way. Pretends to swoon.

I roll my eyes. He's a good-looking bloke and the world's best flirt. But I know him too well to get sucked in by his oven-ready package of abs and shit banter. He's my dude. Just not that kind of dude. "No more tinsel. Give me the big ball things."

"Don't change the subject."

"There was no subject except this pissing tree."

"Last time I checked, trees didn't have bladders, but okay." Galen passes the shoe box of giant balls. "If it's not Bec, who is it? Tinder come through for you?"

"I don't have Tinder."

"Scruff then. You get laid, big daddy?"

"Shut the fuck up." I shoot him a warning look. My sexuality isn't a secret. I'm too lazy to keep up that kind of pretence. But talking about cock is still a no-go around here with anyone that isn't Galen.

Because he's bi too.

Probably why we get lumped together so much.

"It wasn't Scruff," I concede when Galen makes it clear he's not letting it go. "Haven't hooked up in ages."

"What's up with that? Wasn't so long ago that you were spending more time in hotel rooms then you were in your own bed."

"I got used to sleeping alone."

"Like it?"

No. I shrug. "No one puts their cold feet on me or wakes me up with the fucking hair dryer."

"You're all heart, Lo."

I grunt, hoping it's the end of the conversation. But I've given Galen enough that he's now rabidly interested.

He passes me more sparkly balls. Then chocolate stars and bells that aren't going to last the week, let alone till the twenty-fifth of December.

I hang them anyway. Eat three for my trouble.

Galen waggles his brows. "What are you being so fucking coy for? You fall in love or something?"

"What?"

He laughs. "I'm taking the piss, but fuck me, you should see your face."

I don't want to see my face. The amount of time I have to spend chasing my five o'clock shadow off it to stay reasonably clean-shaven, I'm sick of the sight of my miserable mug. "Leave me alone."

"Can't. Boss says we're stuck here till this room is pretty enough for the OAP visit tomorrow."

"Fuck Greeves and his care in the community bullshit." But I mutter it. Our watch manager is a fair man, but if he hears me throwing shade his way I'll be on dinner duty for a month.

Galen laughs. Again. It's his favourite thing to do. Then he falls quiet for a minute or two and I think I've got away with it.

Because I'm a fucking idiot. Turns out he's distracted by scoffing the last of the chocolate stars and hiding the foils. The

68

moment he's done, he's back in my face. "Not still mooning after that festival hook-up, are you?"

Motherfucker. My brother aside, he's the only one who knows about the marshalling gigs I took for cash over the summer. He's also, thanks to a sloppy night out a few months back, the only one who knows I came home from those gigs with a new hobby—daydreaming about wavy blond hair, tattooed hands, and lush lips. "It wasn't a hook-up."

Galen eyes me. "That's not a denial either. You still hung up on that bloke? What happened to *woe is me, I'm never gonna see him again so what's the fucking point?* That shit was tragic, but accurate."

"Was it?"

His brows jump. "Tragic? Yeah. Accurate? I don't know. Something you want to tell me?"

"No."

"Okay, let me rephrase that. Something you don't want to tell me, but you're gonna anyway because I tell you all my shit whether you want to hear it or not?"

That's not entirely true. There's plenty Galen keeps to himself. But he's right about me telling him anyway.

One: the truth is the quickest way to shut him up.

Two: telling him makes it real, and I need that. I've spent too long trying to convince myself what happened with Remy at Greenfest was less than my imagination made it.

Less than it *is*. Because I kissed him again and I can't stop thinking about him.

So really, nothing's changed, right?

Heh. There's logic in there somewhere, but logic isn't my friend when it comes to Remy. My brain short-circuits, my heart flutters, and other parts of my body get way too involved.

I give Galen the briefest recap known to man.

He smirks. Frowns. Then smirks a little more before his face settles somewhere in between. "Why are you in your head about the thing you've been dreaming about all this time?"

"I'm not in my head."

"No? Then why is spacing out over him still making you look like a bulldog shat in your handbag?"

I toss a tree ornament at him. It's made of cardboard and misses his stupid face. I'm tempted to try again with the next one to cross my path, but it's glass and I'm a responsible adult, so I settle for glaring instead. "I always look like that."

"Too true. My point stands, though."

"You didn't make a point." Honestly, Galen is more like my brother than I care to admit. It's why I never go out on the lash with both of them. Can't stand the heat of their pertinent and *terrible* humour. "It's just—"

A shout comes in, the alert siren loud and obnoxious, and as connected to my fucking soul as Remy seems to be.

We drop everything. In motion before thoughts coalesce. We *run*. To our gear, to the engine, and climb into our seats. The whole transition takes minutes. *Seconds*. But it's seismic enough that whatever pearl of introspection I was about to set free gets left by the wayside.

I'm a father. I'm a brother.

Right now, I'm fucking firefighter.

I should be home by seven. But it's late by the time I turn my car up Firefly Hill. The shout was for a pile-up on the motorway. No fires. No smoke and flames. Just a fuckton of twisted metal and enough blood and pain that I need a stiff drink.

Nope. Rule number one, dear brother. You can't erase a bad shift with booze, and trying might mean you'll never stop.

Easy for Locke to say. He's not a firefighter anymore. But I know he's right. We watched our dad prove him right too many times for me to believe anything else.

It's a maudlin thought as I ascend the hill. It's a cold night, clear skies and frost already sparkling in the trees. It makes my home look kind of beautiful, and I latch onto that, hoping it'll overwhelm wherever my trauma-slammed brain wants to go.

Can't deny the glance I send up the hill is deliberate. Self-medicating, almost.

It works, too. The workshop door is down, but there's a sliver of light beneath.

He's here.

Like he always seems to be. Can't think of a time I've searched for that light since Remy arrived and haven't found it. Either he works twenty-four hours a day, or for once, my timing is impeccable.

I tear my gaze away as I come up on my driveway. My headlights sweep my property. At first, nothing jumps out except the sensation that something's different. I roll forward, frowning, flexing my shoulders to ease the strain of an entire shift spent humping hydraulics and loaded stretchers.

Then it dawns on me. *The gate.* It's no longer hanging by its hinges, no use to man or beast. It's upright and hooked to a cast iron bracket screwed into the wall.

Fuck me, it's fixed.

Question is, by who? My brother springs to mind, but he wouldn't come up here without telling me. It's not how we roll. Besides, he's my twin. If it was him, I'd *know*.

So *who*? Because honestly, there's no one else on this earth likes me that much. Especially not my ex-wife who drove into it in the first place.

I steer my car past the gate and park outside my house. My body aches. I heave myself out and find myself gazing up the hill again. Nothing's changed since I looked ten seconds ago, but it feels like everything has.

It was him. I don't know how I know it, but I do.

A group of local Quakers came by the station tonight as we were rolling in from the accident site. I wasn't in the mood to chat, but I took the individual care package one pressed into my hand.

I carry it into the house and poke around in the bag while the kettle boils. It's Christmas-themed, naturally. Mince pies, brandy snaps, and cakes. Sausage rolls and miniature turkey pasties. I set the animal biscuits aside for the boys and take the rest with two mugs of tea back into the cold.

The wind is harsh, but after a day surrounded by motorway traffic, it's cleansing enough that I don't mind it.

I climb the hill. The workshop is quiet, but the hum of activity is strong in the air. The buzz of getting closer to Remy with every crunchy step on the frosted ground.

At the rolling door, I hear a radio playing softly, the local station. It's an ad for Santa's grotto at the garden centre, but I'm lucky enough that my kids don't give a shit about a fat man with a fake beard.

The ad plays out. Wham! kicks in and makes me think of Locke howling out 'Last Christmas' from his Harley in the height of summer, because once upon a time, he liked to be a clown.

He's less ridiculous now.

Still more fun than me, though.

I knock on the door, a light rap of my knuckles. The radio quiets and I hear light footsteps. Then the door's moving, inch by inch, revealing Remy so slowly I almost groan.

His face is worth the wait. His smile when he sees me. "Hello."

"Hey." I hold up the mugs clutched in my other hand. "I brought you some tea."

Remy steps back to wave me inside, then peers beyond me. "Where are the boys?"

"At their mum's. Pick them up after school on Thursday."

He nods and rolls the door down, the snagging rattle I'm used to distinctly absent.

"You fixed that too, eh?"

Remy shrugs and takes a mug from my hand. "It didn't close all the way and it gets mighty cold in here."

I can imagine. I try not to and take a chance instead. "And my gate?"

"Sam told me it's been busted for months. I had some bits in the van, so I screwed them in this afternoon. Took five minutes, mate."

Right. Three hours more like. And why? It makes no sense to me that he'd spend that time on my broken gate. What have I ever done for him?

Remy frowns. "Shit, was it, like, an insurance thing? Did I fuck it up by fixing it?"

"Nah. I'm just...never mind. Thank you. I'd probably never have got round to it. You've saved me a good decade of my ex accusing me of leaving it that way to spite her."

"It was her who knocked it down, though, right?"

"Right."

Remy's frown deepens and I love that he truly doesn't understand. That he's honest enough with his emotions that the complex politics of a broken marriage perplexes him.

"Me and Bec..." I wave my hand. "We're still figuring out how to co-parent without bitching each other to death."

"You don't seem the type to bitch." Remy sips his tea and drifts back to his work bench. "Bad break-up?"

"She fucked her sculpture mentor."

Remy winces. "That'll do it. She break your heart, Papa?"

"Nah." I follow him to the bench and peer at his work. "I was gone a lot with work. Distant and caught up with the boys and family drama when I was home. I'd have cheated on me too."

73

"And you don't get along now?"

I make the half and half gesture again. "We try. But she's busy with work too, and it's hard when you think there's a better parent waiting in the wings while you half arse it. Makes you hypersensitive and critical."

"That's a mature way of looking at it."

"Yeah, well. I'm thirty-eight. Gotta grow up sometime."

If I'm hoping by dropping my age bomb, Remy will drop his, I'm shit out of luck. He just grins and folds his elegant body onto his work stool.

He picks up a small mallet and another tool I don't recognise.

"What's that?"

Remy holds it up. "A mandrel. To make this coin with a hole punched through it into a ring."

He says it like it's ordinary.

Like *he's ordinary*. But as I watch him work with deft fingers and skill, I get another reminder he's nothing of the sort. He shapes the gold coin into a ring, then files out any cracks and marks. Next comes a die and something else I don't recognise, but I don't want to disrupt him, so I watch, sipping my tea and drifting to the Christmas pop filtering from the paint-splattered radio.

It's a while before he holds the ring to the light and inspects it with a critical eye.

"Is it finished?"

"Hmm?" His murmur is absent—maybe he forgot I was here. "Structurally. It still needs engraving and the gemstone set right here." He points to a faint divot. "Amber in this one. It's companion piece has hawk's eye. Wanna see?"

"Fuck yeah."

Remy's expression brightens to one I've never seen before. His coffee-bean eyes warm, and he moves easier than he has since he got here.

He slides from his stool and crosses the shop to a set of metal drawers. From the top drawer, he retrieves a cardboard ring box. Inside is another gold ring, this one smaller, the gold a paler hue, with three tiny blue stones set within it.

It's fucking gorgeous. Rustic, unique, beautiful. I've never seen anything like it. I read the delicate engraving. "Eres mi amor eterno. Spanish?"

"Yeah. The coin too. The other dude must be Hungarian."

"Other dude?"

"They're wedding rings," Remy clarifies. "Rush job from Devon. That's where you're from, right?"

I nod. "It's a big county, though. I don't know many people down there anymore."

Remy puts the Spanish ring back and returns to his workbench. I'm still engrossed enough that I could watch him work all night, but he puts the unfinished piece away and spins to give me his full attention. "What's in the bag?"

"Bag?"

He points at the care package I've abandoned by the door.

I fetch it, explain its origins, and show him the contents. "There's probably enough in here that neither of us will have to cook by the time we get home."

"You haven't been home yet?"

"Only to make tea. Is your place in town?"

Remy takes the bag and claims a sausage roll. He takes a big bite and mimes taking a drink.

I shrug.

He moves to the back door and opens it. Outside on the frosty ground are two bottles of beer.

"It's like you knew I was coming."

Remy swallows and laughs. "Maybe."

He pops the caps from the bottles and hands one over. We clink a cheers and drink. Eat sausage rolls and anything else that takes our fancy while leaning against the wall nearest the wood burner. A quiet settles over us. It's companionable. Soothing. With the doors closed, the world is shut out and I appreciate it more than I care to admit.

Something lingers, though. Something unsaid.

Something *missed*.

I don't get it until I spot a mattress in the corner.

An unrolled sleeping bag.

Fuck. He's sleeping here.

Our makeshift dinner grows heavy in my gut. Disquiet rattles my heart. A collection of unremarkable things become remarkable. The constant light under the door. The van that never moves. Goddamn, how did it take me so long to figure out he's always here because he never leaves?

It's criminally obvious now my brain has kicked into gear. His lack of money and dishevelled appearance. The weariness in his face that wasn't there in the summer.

He got hurt. You'd be tired too if you'd tumbled from the back of a lorry.

Too true. But I have a house and public sector sick pay to fall back on. A twin brother who'd die for me if I needed him to. Who does Remy have?

It twists me up that I have no idea.

It *kills* me that he's spent even one night sleeping in this draughty as fuck workshop that barely has running water, and none of it hot.

I finish my beer and polish off the random Quality Street chocolates from the bottom of the bag.

Remy grins. "Sweet tooth?"

"Bad habits more like. I eat all the kids' crap when they're not around because I can't be arsed to shop more."

"Health is wealth, man."

"Can't be good for your health to be kipping on a stone floor."

For fuck's sake. If I could catch the words as they fall from my stupid mouth and shove them back in.

Remy's smile evaporates. He rubs his lips with the back of his hand and stands off the wall he's been leaning against. "How's that your business?"

There's no aggression in his tone. Only defeat. Like he thinks I'm going to blow up my uncle's phone and get him evicted before the night's out.

As if. I wouldn't do that if he were a stranger. I'd want to know why he was living like this and how to fix it.

But Remy's not a stranger. He's a beautiful, talented, hard-working man who's probably more likely to leave of his own accord than let me help him.

"It's not my business," I say carefully. "As long as you're okay up here."

"Do I look okay?" Remy's grin returns, but it's not sunny this time, it's sardonic, and it doesn't suit him.

My brain flails, searching for a way out of the swamp I've dragged us into.

Words fail me.

I reach for him instead, catching his elbow as he starts to inch away from me, reeling him back in. "You look more than okay to me. And I'm sorry I opened my mouth. I just...I don't want you to be cold."

Remy collides with my chest. I could've avoided it, but I don't want to. I want his hands on me, his lithe body pressed to mine.

I want his smile. The real one.

It takes a second, but Remy settles and I sense him relaxing.

I take a chance and wrap my arms around him, my chin on top of his head.

In my mind, we fit together like Mother Nature made us that way, but I can't help wondering what he's thinking. How I feel when I'm with him is mad alchemy. As though the stars align. Is it like that for him? And then what? I really do drag him back to my fucking cave?

I feel like I could. It's in me, unfurling in my gut. There's something primal in the chemistry that simmers between us. Something I can't ignore as Remy shifts and looks up at me. His brown eyes are so fucking warm. His mouth so kissable.

But he speaks before I can descend on him. He presses a finger to my lips. "Whatever happens, don't try and rescue me."

A thousand counter arguments surge inside me.

His warning gaze keeps them there.

I nod.

Remy adds pressure to my bottom lip, trailing his fingertip back and forth. "I mean it. I don't want your help—I don't need it—and this all falls apart if you force it on me."

He's right, and I know it. But fuck. I want to take him home. To my central heating, my couch, and my fridge that possibly contains something worth eating if I squint hard enough.

But I want him in my bed too, for reasons far beyond keeping him warm for his health, and that's where the lines blur. And they can't. Not if he says so. It's his life, not mine.

I grasp his wrist, pulling his hand away from my face. "Can I make a counter offer?"

"No."

"Please?"

"Fucking hell, don't look at me like that."

"Like what?"

Remy kind of scowls, but he's laughing too. "You're too cute. All right. I'm listening."

"How about I stay out of your shit if you promise to come stay with us if it snows?"

"Snows?"

"Yeah. As in, the white stuff everywhere. It's so much colder up here when it's thick on the ground. I couldn't sleep at night knowing you were basically kipping in the arctic without a tent."

He rolls his eyes and nods.

It's a small victory, but I happen to know there's a harsh weather front rolling in. Station manager showed a radar picture at briefing this morning. How hard it hits remains to be seen, but extracting that soundless promise from Remy settles me.

Makes me brave. Or stupid, depending on how the next ten seconds play out. "Can I offer one other thing?"

Remy sighs. "If it's money, I'll burn it."

"How about a hot shower? Anytime you like? I'm not going to be home much the next few days, I can leave you a key."

"Why—"

It's my turn to silence him with a finger to his lips. "You fixed my gate. I'm offering you use of my bathroom in return. That's a fair exchange, no rescuing in sight."

Conflict rages in Remy's eyes. I hold firm a moment, then let him speak.

"You don't know me. Why the hell would you want me in your house when you're not there?"

I give him the only answer I can think of. "I *want* to know you."

Whether it's enough or not, I have no idea. But it seems to shift something in Remy. He puts his hands on my chest and pushes me.

For a hot second, I think he's pushing me *away*. Then I realise he's right there with me.

My back hits the wall. I let it happen. Let Remy manhandle me with his smaller frame, cos let me tell you, he's every bit as strong as me in any way that matters.

He kisses me, but it's not slow and sweet this time. It's not gentle. It's rough and biting, and it steals my breath.

I flatten against the wall, opening my arms. Remy steps into them, his hands still on my chest, and he kisses me harder, his tongue slipping between my lips.

Fuck. Me. I groan, I can't help it, this deep, strangled mess of sound, and I grip his hip with one hand, the other cupping the nape of his neck.

My hand is big enough that my thumb finds his jaw, my fingers splayed wide. I anchor him closer, holding him in place, and he *shudders*, snatching a sharp breath.

He likes that.

Noted. I'm always careful with my overbearing size, but I've always longed for a lover who enjoys my strength and heavy weight.

Maybe I've found him.

I deepen the kiss. Another pleasured shiver rattles Remy and it goes straight to my overheated blood, pushing it faster round my body. Pushing it *lower*, to my already straining cock.

Suddenly, the fact he has a mattress on the floor doesn't seem such a bad thing.

I don't push him onto it, though. I kiss him until we run out of air, then I reluctantly draw back. "I should go."

Remy licks his lips. He's so close that I feel his tongue as it snakes in and out and I can't stop myself kissing him again.

We lose more minutes to each other. The radio starts kicking out The Carpenters. It's romantic as hell until the chirpy Sleigh Ride beat kicks in.

Then I laugh.

Remy laughs too and everything is perfect except the grim reality that I have to leave him in this cold, draughty box and go spend the night in my big warm bed all by myself.

I stifle a sigh as Remy shuffles back. I'm kiss-drunk on him. Even without the mattress-on-the-floor situation, leaving him feels impossible, especially with no clue when I'll see him again —for real, not a glimpse up the damn hill. "Um…"

That articulate brilliance earns me another dose of Remy's sparkly grin. I soak it up, storing it for later when I'm alone, and try again, but damn, it's hard. I've never asked a dude out in my life. Never wanted to. My sole experience at relationships is a marriage that blew up in my face. Since then, I've had no time or patience for anything that isn't instant gratification.

No-strings fucking.

And *lord*, I want to fuck Remy. So much. But there's a buried-deep part of me reaching for something else. "I'm working a day shift tomorrow. You wanna do something after?"

Remy's brows rise. "Like what?"

"Get a drink. Bag of chips. Maybe a walk."

Honestly, even if I didn't know he was strapped for cash and doesn't give much of a fuck for fancier things, I've just let slip my ideal date. I don't like fancy things either. I like chips. I like beer. And I love being outside with someone who makes me feel good.

If I can be that for Remy, just for one night...yeah, I'll be happy.

He doesn't seem to know what to say. I reach into my pocket and find the loose key I picked up on my way out of the house.

I toss it to him. "There's a pub behind the old chalk plant at the bottom of the hill. I'll probably go there after work. If you don't wanna join me, feel free to use the bathroom while I'm gone."

"I never agreed to that."

"You don't have to agree to anything, Rem. Just know all these things exist if you need them. Or...if you want them. Night, mate."

I leave before he can answer. It still feels wrong, but I'll see him tomorrow. I know it.

Because he's as hooked on those kisses as I am.

I want to meet Logan for that pint. I want to huddle in the corner of a quiet boozer and get gently drunk with him. As far as my current bucket list goes, it's top-tier.

At the bottom? Letting myself into his house and using his shower because now *he knows* I'm squatting like a tramp in his uncle's workshop. But I can't have one without doing the other. I'm a humble dude, but date night without taking a shower is too basic even for me.

Fuck's sake. I know I should be grateful he reacted with a spare key rather than grassing me up to Uncle Marr, but really? Why does the universe have to do me like this?

Ruminating over that keeps me company most of the day. I finish the wedding bands and pack them up ready for posting. Arrange a courier for the copper worktop. I'm banging out my third pendant when I realise I'm running out of time.

I dig clean clothes from my van and shove them into a bag with my mostly empty shampoo bottle. Then I inhale the last of the treats Logan left behind last night—along with the imprint of his lips on mine—and set off down the hill.

It's a shorter trek than the one I'd been planning before Logan spotted my sleeping bag. But it pisses me off. I don't want to be the dude he feels sorry for. The dude who needs *help*. If I hadn't fixed his gate, I'd be schlepping myself down to the community centre to use the showers there, and I'm too irritated to feel thankful I don't have to.

The key Logan gave me is for the back door. I hurdle the side gate, glad he has no neighbours to think I'm a burglar, and land in his garden.

It's a big space with a bunch of levels, un-landscaped and kind of wild with crazy tall trees and bramble bushes. There's a football goal too, surrounded by half-deflated balls. A shed with some bikes.

The back door is weathered with peeling paint. Pretty sure I could jimmy it open without the key, but I'm not about that life. I unlock it and slip inside, finding myself in Logan's cosy kitchen.

Without him guarding the stove, it's not the instant shot of warmth it was the other night.

I don't linger. I leave my boots at the door and hustle to the narrow stairs.

At the top, I find myself face-to-face with Logan's bedroom. The door is open and his big wooden bed is right there, made but messy, his bedside table loaded with toy cars, a coffee mug, and a couple of picture frames. Curiosity burns a path to my soul, but I don't let myself stare too long. He didn't offer me his shower so I could snoop on him.

The bathroom is past a room I assume belongs to the boys. There's a big old bath filled with more toy cars, and a shower cubicle.

I set my bag down, take my coat off, and pull my socks from my feet. The clothes from my upper body follow, but I hesitate at my jeans and underwear. Being naked in Logan's house feels weird.

Wouldn't if he was here.

Probably not. Hopefully he'd be naked too, and I'd be

distracted by his warm skin and solid muscle. His cut chest and his cock.

Bet he's huge.

Man, I need to stop thinking about his cock. If there's one thing weirder than being naked in Logan's house, it's having a lonely boner too.

I force my thoughts into the least sexy thing I can think of. The rent payment I'm going to send Logan's uncle in a few weeks, despite him not wanting it for a while yet. Sales are good, and my productivity is even better. If nothing goes wrong, I'll have enough by the end of the year to pay him a few months ahead.

What if it does go wrong, though? What if you lose all your tools again, or—

Nope. Not doing that. I unbutton my jeans and shove them away, hooking my boxers over my semi and kicking them aside too.

The shower is old enough that I don't need a YouTube video to work it. I crank it on and step under the spray, and the moment the hot water hits my skin, my pride goes out the window. Fuck it if Logan thinks I'm a hobo, I'm staying right here for the rest of my life.

I close my eyes and let the water beat down on my neck and shoulders, the constant ache fading away. Even the tightness in my chest shifts, the steam clearing lungs that are fed up of being cold. It's so good. I brace my hands on the tiles, the water lulling me into a trance. I almost fall asleep.

But as soothing as Logan's shower is, it's got nothing on him, and I have half an hour to get my shit together and hoof it down the hill to meet him.

I get clean and leave the magic hot water behind. I swap my grubby work clothes for jeans and a vintage Glastonbury T-shirt, and clean up the bathroom.

It doesn't take much to leave it as I found it. Logan's house is clean, but gloriously cluttered.

I love it.

Downstairs, I head for my boots, but the *drip-drip* of a leaking tap derails me. I follow the sound to the downstairs cloakroom, the basin hidden by more boxes of Christmas decorations. I push them aside and assess the tap. Unlike most things I've encountered recently, the problem is simple and easy to fix.

It takes all of five minutes and it won't bring Logan anywhere near as much pleasure as his hot shower did me, but it's all I have.

I move the boxes back.

One of them is open and loaded with wrapping paper and glittery Christmas bows.

I steal one and stick it to the mended tap. With the boxes in front of it, he might not see it for a while, but I guess that's part of the fun.

Unless he's never noticed the tap dripping in the first place.

I chew on that as I lace my boots and let myself out of Logan's house, locking up and triple-checking behind me. It's a theory that doesn't suit him. He's no domestic god, but something not working the way it should...he'd see it.

He saw it in me.

I hike down the hill. The old chalk plant is at the left fork at the bottom. I've never noticed a pub behind it, but when I get there, there it is, a quaint old inn that's been repurposed as a microbrewery.

The pub part is small, not much bigger than a living room, and every patron inside—bar one—is a middle-aged white man nursing dark ale. With my damp goldilocks and tattooed hands, I stand out, but no one seems to notice me.

Not even Logan, who's in the corner, texting, and frowning as though his phone has deeply offended him.

His beer glass is empty. I go to the bar and point over my shoulder. "Two of them."

The barman nods. Pours two pints of something dark enough to put me on my arse, and takes my money.

It's cheaper than I expect. Can't deny that thrills me.

I take the beer to Logan's table and slide one in front of him. He jerks his head up, blinking.

It's cute. I almost ruffle his hair, but settle for knocking my fist to his bulging bicep instead. "All right?"

His handsome face relaxes into a slow grin. "Am now. Raining, is it?"

He gestures to my shower-damp hair.

I send him a glare with zero malice or heat. "Monsoon, mate. Didn't you hear it?"

"Nope. Made a point of not listening to anything that wasn't that old dude asking me what beer I want."

"Sounds like you've had a day."

Logan wraps a hand around his pint and swallows a healthy measure before he answers me with a shrug. "Bec's on my case."

"The boys' mum?"

"Yeah. I have to make something with them for school. It's due soon and I haven't even started it yet."

"What is it?"

"A farm? A barn? Something like that. Billy mentioned shoeboxes, but he doesn't really give a shit, so I can't rely on that."

"What's Sam saying?"

"Nothing, but Bec said he was crying yesterday because he's worried he won't have one." Guilt flickers in Logan's eyes. "I don't mean to forget things, you know? I'm caught between two worlds most of the time, and they're both a lot."

He's not wrong. Firefighter. Single dad. Man, I'm not built for that kind of stress. "Hey, my mum used to say if me and my sister were both still alive at the end of the day, she'd done her job well."

Logan drinks more beer then sets his glass down. "Older sister?"

"Younger. She's twenty-three."

"And that makes you...?"

"Older than her."

Logan nudges my foot with his, apparently as close to kicking me as he's prepared to go.

My counter move is curling my leg around his. My reward is his wider smile and Pistol Annies playing in the background. It's cheesy as fuck, but still better than Sleigh Ride. "I'm twenty-six if you really want to know."

"Really?" Logan's brows jump. "I thought you might be younger. You, uh, looked young when I met you, but the facial hair...I like it."

I scrub a hand through the mess on my jaw. It's not the beard I know he's capable of if he doesn't shave for three hours. It's dark blond, close to my skin, and in six months' time, it'll probably look exactly the same, but if he likes it, I'll keep it forever.

Forever. What planet are you on?

I shake myself, silencing the negativity that took root inside me that hazy night I fell from the rig. It's not natural. It's not *mine*. I'm not gonna let it ruin this precious time with the honest, sweet man beside me.

Logan watches me process and pushes my untouched beer towards me. "Sorry. I've only had one, but I'm a clumsy fucker with words at the best of times."

"Bet you're not."

"Not what?"

"A clumsy *fucker*."

Logan sends me a simmering stare. It draws me in. I want to reach across the table and kiss him.

87

I want more than that.

So much more I can't let myself picture it.

Not now.

Not here.

Not *yet*.

If We Make it Through December plays out. Cara Dillon takes over and her voice is chill enough to help contain the smoulder growing inside.

I drink the dark beer. It's bitter and smoky, and tastes of cocoa. I wonder what it would taste like on Logan's lips.

Or if he's thinking about that too.

He breaks the spells first, his deep chuckle rich and smooth. "You're gonna get me in trouble, sitting all the way over there looking like that."

"If I was any closer, I'd be in your lap."

"Say it like it's a bad thing. I dare you."

"I tell no lies."

"Good." Logan drains his beer and stands. "Hold that thought, yeah?"

For how long, he doesn't say. He heads to the bar and orders more drinks. Disappears into the gents while they're being poured. I want to follow him *so bad*, but the quaint little micropub isn't that kind of place.

I tip more dark beer down my throat. It settles in my stomach, overwhelming the packet rice I ate for breakfast. With business picking up, I can afford more food now, but I haven't got round to it yet. Somehow, it never seems important until it's shit o'clock at night and my belly tries to eat itself.

Beer has calories, right?

I keep drinking. My glass is empty when Logan comes back and swaps it out.

"What's your sister's name?"

"Hollie."

Logan sits down. Wraps his leg around mine again. "Are you close?"

I shake my head. "She's still in Port Talbot. I left ten years ago."

"When you were sixteen?"

"Yup. Jumped on a festival bus and never came home."

"What about your parents?"

"My dad died when I was twelve. My mam doesn't give a shit about anything except the bingo."

Logan winces. "Sorry."

"Nah, it's cool. That kind of family is normal to me. I don't know any different. I had a boyfriend once with three brothers, two sisters, and parents who were all up in his business all the time. Scared the shit out of me."

"Ran a mile, eh?"

"Broke the sound barrier on the way out."

Logan pushes his sleeves up his forearms. Dark hair dusts his skin, a small tattoo on the underside I've never seen up close before.

It's a vintage lock.

"My brother has the key on his arm," he explains, catching me looking. "We thought it was profound as fuck when we were eighteen."

"It's nice that you're close enough to share ink. You talk to him much?"

"In my head?" Logan taps his temple. "Every ten minutes. In practice, every week or so, but he speaks to the boys more when he calls. They love him."

"You miss him." It's not a question.

Logan nods anyway. "We haven't lived in the same county for a decade, and he's never lived here, but I still think every knock at the door might be him."

I can't imagine what that's like—to be so connected to my

sister that she's in my thoughts every day. Half the time I forget she exists, and I know she feels the same.

Families, man.

We drink more beer and peel back the paper on each other. I tell Logan about festival life and how I learned to dance with fire.

He tells me that being a firefighter is what Halliwell men do. "My dad, my uncles, my brother. It's in our blood."

"You want that for your boys too?"

"I want them to be happy. Don't care how they get there. Hey, are you hungry?"

Hungry, and more than a little merry. I admit the first, hide the second.

Logan makes good on his promise of a bag of chips, the salt and pepper kind from the Chinese place on the corner. They're salty and spicy and I can't stop eating them.

I eat Logan's too, while he's in the shop buying more.

He grins. "I love watching you eat."

"Because I drop it all down myself?" I brush salt and five-spice from my jacket.

"No." Logan helps, hands lingering. "Because I want to lick that salt off your lips."

His smile is as buzzed as I feel. Not drunk, just charged from a couple of beers and some loaded company.

Not sure if he really wants to lick my fingers in the street, but I won't stop him if he tries.

He doesn't. Instead he takes my hand and starts towing me in the general direction of Firefly Hill.

I'm okay with that. I mean, I'm in no hurry to be without him all night long, but I like walking with him. Logan, he's so big and strong, but now he's put his phone away there's a lightness to him tonight, and it's infectious. I smile even when we're not talking, and I can't remember the last time I smiled for no tangible reason.

Once we get a little way up, Firefly Hill is a place that belongs to just us. There's nothing here except his house and the workshop. It's a cold night. The scattered woodland sparkles in the frost. Owls call, foxes scream. It's like the town below and the city beyond don't exist, until Logan slows to a stop and sets his hands on my shoulders, turning me around.

"You can see the entire northside of the city from up here."

I follow his gaze, taking in the distant, twinkling lights, and a cathedral spire. "I don't like cities anymore."

"Me neither. I only work there because the pay is better."

"Bet you earn that extra money."

"Some days."

It's not a line of conversation that ever opens Logan up. I lean back into him, absorbing his warmth, and close my eyes.

He presses wind-cold lips to my neck.

I shiver. God, he's so good at the simple things. It's so fucking easy. I tip my head. He kisses me a little harder, his tongue hot and sweet against my skin, and I feel that kiss *everywhere*, from my toes to my scalp. From my lips to the blood pooling south in my groin.

Logan rumbles out a soft hum and eases me around again. "I could stand out here all night, but I kinda want to be somewhere warmer with you."

"Kinda?"

"A lotta, actually."

I stretch up to capture his mouth, grinning against his lips at first, but my smile fades as the kiss deepens, growing in intensity with every brush of lips and snatched breath. We're on a precipice. Until now, this has been all we are. If we wind up in his big bed, or rolling around on my old mattress, everything changes.

Logan slides his hands under my coat and my clothes. His hands skim my ribs and my limbs grow slack.

Fuck, I want him.

And I know he wants me. I can feel it in the anaconda he's packing in those jeans.

His touch entrances me. I stop thinking about anything else. We kiss until he pulls back and takes my hand again. His house is closer. The stubborn idiot I carry inside wants to drag him to the workshop for no other reason than his house is so nice I won't want to leave, but I let him have his way.

He's too cute to refuse.

Inside, it dawns on me how cold I am. Rather, it dawns on my nervous system.

Logan unbuttons my coat, tracking the shivers that wrack me, concern knitting his dark brows. "Hey, why don't you take another shower? Warm them bones up."

"Ta, but I'm all good."

"Uh-huh. Hold out your hands."

"No."

"Why not?"

Because they're jerking so much I'll probably punch one of us in the face.

I frown instead, matching his expression. But he doesn't hold his for long. His handsome face softens and he draws me in for a hug.

"How about this? Go take a hot shower while I make tea and crank the heating. Then I'll get you all dirty again."

This man has a unique way of being so fucking sweet and *filthy* at the same time. It's so potent it should be a weapon, and I'm powerless against it.

My frown remains, but I find myself in the bathroom anyway, slipping under the hot stream for the second time today.

I don't need to scrub my skin this time. Just warm myself up enough that he stops worrying about anything more than what he truly wants. I stay until I'm no longer quaking, then jump out and wrap my waist in the same towel I used this afternoon.

It's slightly damp, but I don't care. The hot water and the heat seeping out of the radiators, combined with the knowledge that Logan's waiting for me...goddamn, it's impossible to feel cold. It blows my mind that I ever did.

I hear his footsteps on the stairs.

My clothes are on the tiles, a beacon of the last thing standing between me and him.

I step over them and open the door.

Logan

I've seen Remy's bare chest before, but that was then. When he was a stranger dancing on dry grass, twirling a fire hazard above his head.

Now, he's a man I've kissed too many times to count, and he's in my house, on my landing, with nothing but a towel hiding his body from me.

I'm holding mugs of tea neither of us wants. I abandon them on the windowsill and close the distance between us.

Remy tracks my every step, bottom lip caught between his teeth.

I swipe it free and kiss him. Just once.

Then I step back and take him in properly.

He has sun-kissed tattooed skin. Paler than the summer, but still a body that's spent months and months outside. There are scars too—little nicks here and there. A whopper of a scuff on his back that I can tell came from eating dirt off the back of a lorry. It's lost its pigment, growing white with age. I skate my fingers over it and watch goosebumps prickle his skin.

I'm so hard right now. Fuck, I've been hard all night, my dick pressing against my zip, fighting for freedom.

I hook my fingers into the pendant that hangs around his

neck. It feels like part of him. I want to know how long he's worn it. I want to know *everything*.

But first...

I let the pendant drop to his chest. He has a smattering of hair there. Not as much as me, but still enough to press every button I have, darkening as it descends his lean abdomen, disappearing under the towel.

The towel has to go.

I hold his gaze and reach for the fold on his hip, giving him every chance to stop me.

He doesn't. I pull the end free and the towel drops to the floor.

It's dark on the landing, and my vision is swimming with so much fucking desire it's hard to see. To accept how goddamn beautiful he is. I wrap one hand around his jaw and let the other ghost lower, trailing my fingertips down his belly, skimming his cock as it rises to meet me.

"Fuck." Remy shudders and shuts his eyes. "How do you make me feel so much when you're hardly touching me?"

Because there's something between us I can't explain. That no one can. It's a biological, spiritual reaction that can't be contained. And I'm not going to try.

Not tonight.

I want his skin on mine.

I want him splayed out beneath me.

Lucky for me, my bedroom is two steps away.

I guide Remy backwards and to my bed.

At the edge, he stops me. "You're wearing too many clothes."

Easily fixed. I reach over my shoulder and grip my shirt, hauling it over my head. In the dark, we're chest to chest, and Remy goes for my belt buckle.

He gets it open and pops the button at my waistband, the other hand moving to the zip.

My jeans disappear. The black boxers I grabbed from my locker at work. Pretty sure they have a hole in, but Remy doesn't seem to notice. He pushes me back to get a better look at me, gaze fixed on my cock as he expels a shaky breath. "You're big everywhere, eh?"

"If you say so."

He doesn't need to. I know I have a big dick, but that's all it is. A piece of flesh that can hurt people if I don't pay attention.

PSA: I always pay attention.

I reclaim my place pressed up against Remy and kiss him again. Naked, it hits different. Heat flares in my nerves, buzzing in my veins. I don't know what the night holds for us, but I'm on the edge already. Practiced control will keep me there, but the honest truth is it won't take much to send me catapulting into space.

Remy digs his fingers into my arms. He has short, blunt nails, but the pressure is enough to make my eyes roll.

I need him.

We're still at the edge of the bed.

I push Remy down, then drive my hands beneath him and heave him up the bed.

His eyes flash and I remember that he likes it when my touch turns a little rougher.

I cover him with my body, nudging his legs apart to make room for me. Again, it's a perfect fit, but we're not going to fuck tonight. I want to, *so much*. But this feels like more. And I want it to last.

Doesn't stop me slotting our dicks together and starting a slow grind.

Remy licks his lips, eyes hooded. "Did you know how good that would feel before you did it?"

"With you? No. My best guess didn't even come close."

I manoeuvre us a little, changing the angle. Pleasure builds in my gut, but I stave it off, keeping it so fucking slow I make my own eyes roll.

A groan rips free of my lungs. I bite Remy's neck and drag my teeth down his chest, revelling in the arch of his spine.

I want him in my mouth.

So I take him, dipping down the bed and swallowing him whole.

Remy groans, body jerking.

I hold in place and work my tongue up and down his length, finding the sensitive spots that make him fight my grip on him.

Make him gasp and shudder.

His every sound stokes the inferno inside me. I think I could come just listening to him fall apart, but I'm not ready for this to end. I drag him to the edge and ease off, only to pull him right back, over and over, until I release him from my mouth and sit back on my heels.

Remy catches his breath, eyes screwed shut, throat exposed.

I wait, blood pumping, but with a calm that's eluded me for months. Maybe even years.

"Can I touch you?"

I refocus. Remy has opened his eyes. His gaze is hot and hazy, chest rising and falling with breath that's a little too fast. "Where do you want to touch me?"

Remy's stare falls to my cock. He sits up in the same moment I reach for him, not that I think he needs my help.

I guide him upright anyway and despite the fact I've had his dick in my mouth the last ten minutes, it hits me all over again that we're both naked.

More blood surges south. My cock does this little bob and Remy smirks. "All right there?"

I shrug, unapologetic. "You're so fucking hot."

"Back at you, Papa."

Yeah. Okay. My dick likes that too.

I take Remy's wrist and steer his hand where I want him. He doesn't need my help with that either, but I like how it feels, holding him while he holds me, feeling his tendons flex and stretch while he does something fucking *sorcerous* to my cock.

Remy is a dexterous motherfucker. There's a tiny part of me that believes I have some control over this, but the truth is I'm just bigger, and Remy is letting me have my way.

The pressure points in his palm tell another story. The grip in his deft fingers. He's gonna make me explode and there's nothing I can do about it unless I find the willpower to stop him.

I expel a rough breath and fight the surge in my nerves. The expanding bloom of pleasure in my gut. I find his hooded and heady gaze and lose myself in it. "That's so fucking good."

Remy moves closer, still working me, and kisses my neck, light and teasing, flicking his tongue over my skin.

I shudder. God, I need to come. But I need more of him first. Fuck, I just need him with me.

It's not a complicated thing in my mind, to be with a man. I've been doing it since I was seventeen. I'm not as adept at rolling through my sexuality as my brother is, but this part is everything. The rising heat. The puzzle pieces that come together. Sometimes the final picture isn't that great, but I already know with Remy it's going to be a fucking masterpiece.

I find the composure to rearrange us, rising to my knees in the same moment I tug him to his. I cradle the back of his head with one hand and kiss him, still fucking his hand. But I want him to fuck mine too, so we can come together.

He's still hot and wet from my mouth. I bring his cock to mine and they rub together, the friction mind-numbing.

Remy gasps and digs his fingers into my shoulder. A vibration travels through him and into me, and my bedroom grows suddenly airless.

We become the sum of our physical attraction. Low moans

and gravelled sighs. The slip and slide of our hands. I hook my arm around Remy's torso, anchoring us together, and sweat builds on our skin.

"Fuck," Remy whispers. "I can't...fuck."

His legs quake and a rush ripples through me. I'm transfixed by him. Obsessed. Even more than I was when I watched him dance in that sun-baked field. In the dark of my bedroom, he's as ethereal as he was then, but this isn't pure and seraphic. This is dirty, hot, and primal, and I can't contain the rough sound that escapes me. "You're gonna make me come."

Remy groans and drops his head to my shoulder. I miss his face. His eyes. His full lips. But god, the way his whole body jerks is gonna kill me.

I can't tell who comes first. Just that it happens. To both of us.

A moan wrenches from deep in my chest. Wet warmth coats my fingers and Remy sways on his knees.

Holding him up distracts me from falling into a heap of my own. What we've done...it's basic. It's stuff I was doing when I was a teenager. But I've just come harder than I...fuck, then I ever have, and I need a minute to process.

Remy breathes hard against my shoulder. He's shaking. Or maybe it's me.

Doesn't matter. I keep him steady until he can raise his head, and the stunned satisfaction I find in his eyes matches mine.

I kiss him, sucking his bottom lip briefly into my mouth. "Good, eh?"

Remy shakes his head into a long blink. "What did you just do to me?"

"Same thing you did to me."

"If that's true, you're fucking welcome. Have you got a—?"

"Yeah. Hang on." I release him and slide off the bed. My legs are wobbly as fuck and I like it.

In the bathroom, I wash my hands and grab a wet flannel.

I carry it back to Remy. He cleans up, then takes it back to the bathroom.

He's gone a minute or so.

I give him space and flop onto my back, staring at the ceiling. I was a little drunk when we left the pub, but the beer buzz is long gone now. In its place, I have Remy slaking my synapses clean of all worry. I feel...fresh? Maybe? It's the wrong word, and perhaps I just mean wired.

But I've never felt like this after a hook-up before. I've never felt so fucking good after *anything*.

Remy comes back to the doorway. He's holding his clothes and has the air of a man about to leave.

Not happening. Deep down, the fact that I don't want him to sleep on the cold workshop floor is definitely a factor. But most of all, I don't want to let him go.

I don't want this night to end, but if it does, I want it to end with him in my bed. "Stay."

"Hmm?" Dazed, Remy blinks. "What?"

I sit up and hold out my hand. "Whatever you're thinking, stop. Spend the night with me, please?"

The seconds tick by, the awkward soundtrack to the cogs turning in Remy's brain. He scrubs a hand down his face, squeezing his eyes shut, conflict raging loud and clear, even if he thinks he's hiding it from me.

I get up and pad across the dark room to him. He doesn't stop me as I take his clothes and set them on the chest of drawers by the door.

Doesn't flinch as I take his face in my hands. "Compromise. Come lie with me a while. If you still want to go in a bit, I'll walk you home."

Remy opens his eyes. They roll as I thread my fingers into his messy hair and massage the nape of his neck. He's tight there, probably from hunching over all day.

I work out a knot and let him ruminate. Kiss his temple and wait for him to relax.

Eventually, he leans into me with a low sigh. "You could charm the birds from the trees, you know that?"

"As long as I'm charming you, nothing else matters."

Remy is a quiet sleeper. He lets me curve around him from behind, one hand on his injured hip, the other buried in his hair, and knocks out, and he doesn't move all night. Doesn't snore, cough, or mutter.

Doesn't so much as fucking twitch.

I know this because I wake up every ten minutes to convince myself that having him in my bed isn't a figment of my imagination.

Also, that he's still alive.

The second one's a joke. Mostly. But I'm so used to co-sleeping being a disruptive experience that when he doesn't keep me up all night, I decide to disrupt myself.

Couldn't make it up.

I wake early, brain thick with scattered dozing. Remy is still in my arms, lashes like fans on his cheeks, hand clasped around my wrist.

He's reaching up and back to do that. I fret that it's hurting his shoulder and detach him long enough to lower his arm.

Nothing changes. He sleeps on like a gift from God, and I can't stop staring. Or running my fingers through his hair. My body is alive with what we did to each other last night, blood humming with desire, my cock already hard. But nothing on earth would make me wake him, so I stare instead, fully entertained before my bladder ruins the party.

I ease back from Remy and slip out of bed. Find a clean pair of underwear from the towering basket of doom by the door, and pad to the bathroom. I take a piss and shove a toothbrush in my mouth, multitasking by wiping Sam's graffiti off the mirror at the same time.

A shower crosses my mind, but I don't want to be away from Remy that long.

Not that he notices I'm gone. I shuffle back to find him still fast asleep and only the fact that I'm *starving* stops me crawling back under the duvet.

I mean, I can live with the noise in my belly, but what if he's hungry too?

Fussing about it drives me downstairs. I'm not much of a domestic god but I keep breakfast stuff in the house even when the boys aren't here. I have sausages, hash browns, and bread that's seen better days.

I toast it and plate it up with the grilled bangers and baked hash browns. Remy put hot sauce on his sausages last time. I stick it under my arm and take it with the two plates upstairs.

He's still sleeping. I put the plates down and go back for the tea I need to function.

Back upstairs, I abandon it all and lie beside Remy to rouse him. I can't tell if he's one of those people who snaps to alertness or if it'll take a while, but I'm prepared for both.

I brush his hair back from his face, letting my fingertips ghost over his high cheekbone.

At first, nothing happens.

Then his breathing shallows and his eyes flutter open, and I lean back, giving him space, in case he's forgotten he's in my bed.

That he's *naked* in my bed.

Remy's face scrunches up. It's cute, and somehow makes him hotter. His gaze darts around the room before it settles on me, and finally, he smiles. "I'm alive. Thought I might've come so hard I'd expire in my sleep."

I'm not about to admit I checked he was still breathing

more than once. Nope. Nopetty nope. I rub a hand over his forearm, then reach for the tea. "I can swap it for coffee if you want."

"Nah. Whatever's good."

Remy accepts the mug. I help him sit up, ignoring his amusement, and hand him a plate.

His face brightens for real. "Wow. Maybe I did die after all."

"This is your idea of heaven?"

His reply is cut off by my phone alarm. Since the death march lecture I gave him a few weeks back, Billy's changed it to Steeleye Span, and he's set the volume to louder than hell.

Little shit. I silence the phone and flick the radio on instead. It's a local station. More Christmas pop and a gentle debate about traffic-calming measures. Keeps me company when I'm alone for days on end.

Fuck. I'm turning into my dad.

It's a sobering thought. Literally. I stare off, lost by it, until Remy pokes me and hands me the other plate. "All right?"

"Yeah. Sorry."

Remy eyes me. "You gave me the hand job of my life *and* breakfast. You've got no apologies in the bank till next Christmas."

The idea of him being around next Christmas is enough to snap me out of my daze. I pass him cutlery and we eat breakfast in bed. Drink tea and listen to the radio while a wet winter storm picks up outside.

When we're done, Remy steals my boxers and takes the plates downstairs. I hear him clearing up and have half a mind to stop him, but I stay in bed listening to the wind howl and rain batter the windows, and I can't make myself move.

A little while later, I hear the shower turn on. The taps. The bathroom cabinet open and close. It isn't the herd of elephants the boys' bring home, but I like the sound of another person in the house. Somehow, I feel warmer.

"I stole a toothbrush from the box."

I open my heavy eyes. Remy's in the doorway, hair damp again, another towel around his waist, and a dinosaur toothbrush wedged between his lips. "Fuck, sorry. I meant to give you one last night."

Remy waggles his brows and disappears again. If he comes back with clothes on, I'll probably cry, but he doesn't.

He comes back *naked* and crawls under the covers.

His feet are cold.

I wrap my legs around his. My arms around the rest of him and hold him close.

He doesn't say anything.

Neither do I, and it's perfect.

We drift for a while. Almost asleep, but not quite. He's so peaceful like this, so fucking tranquil, that my mind switches off. There's no night shift looming over me. Nothing I've forgotten that's going to bite me in the arse later.

There's nothing else at all. It's him and me, and time seems like something for other people.

I don't know how much has passed when I realise we're moving together, soft, undulating circles, each pass a shiver of hot friction.

My lips are at his throat, my hands roaming his lean torso. He hooks a leg over my hip. Bites my shoulder. I groan and we ascend into something slow and wicked.

"Fuck, Remy."

He swallows the words with a kiss, hot and breathless, pulling me over him, my weight pinning him to the mattress.

We grind together until we both come, and you know what?

It's the best lazy day I've ever had.

Remy

I spend sixteen hours in Logan's bed. I should be working. He should be resting before his night shift. But we spend all day messing around instead. We come more times than I can count and I have no tangible regrets.

Parting ways rushes up on us. One minute it's midday and we have all the time in the world, the next it's five o'clock and I'm trying to persuade him not to walk me up the hill.

I win. Just. But only because he's running late and he needs to rescue his car from the pub car park. "Go." I push him down the hill.

He plants his feet. "But your hair's wet."

Because we showered together and he blew me under the spray. Not sure how clean that makes me, or how relevant it is to the conversation, but I'll take his sweetness all day long.

I kind of did.

Logan leaves. He doesn't kiss me goodbye. Instead, he squeezes my hand and gives me a scrap of paper with his phone number on, and somehow that hits me harder.

Goddamn him.

Fuck, I have so much to do.

I trudge up the hill and let myself into the workshop. Overnight, I've taken eleven necklace orders and an enquiry for copper penny floor tiles.

I'm not much of a wordsmith, but I fudge a reply, collate the orders, and plug Logan's number into my phone. Then, because I'm in a good mood, I call my mum.

She doesn't answer.

Shocker.

It's not enough to dim the lights, though. I set my phone on the workbench and get to work, ploughing through orders and packing up parcels for the post office tomorrow.

Before I know it, it's the middle of the night and I'm barrelling towards the witching hour.

It's become my least favourite time since winter hit. It's the coldest. The loneliest. Most nights, I wake up shivering and stiff and huddle in front of the stove until I thaw out enough to go back to sleep.

But that doesn't happen tonight. I'm wide awake, and with the memory of Logan's touch still searing my skin, I'm far from cold.

I can't stop thinking about him. His big, warm hands. His deep green eyes and rough groan when he comes.

It blows my mind that we didn't actually fuck. I feel like we did, I'm that consumed by him.

Text him.

It's not my thing—texting. I want to squeeze his hand back. Welcome him home. Make him breakfast, and soothe him to sleep with the gentle touch he put me into a coma with last night.

Can I type six words into a message to express that?

Not a chance.

Also, I don't have a home, so...

That's the thought that finally tanks my mood. Logan's bed is as big and comfortable as he is, and he wanted me in it before he found out I was on my arse up here. But he's a good person. A kind soul. It's hard not to imagine he wouldn't be cooking me breakfast and making me tea regardless.

I abandon my phone and retreat to the mattress in the corner. I'm too wired to sleep, but I sit in front of the stove anyway, blowing on my hands, gaze flickering to my cracked Samsung every two minutes.

It feels like a fire that isn't lit properly, all smoke and no heat. A half done job. An itch that won't go away until I stand and snatch the phone from the workbench.

Logan's number is still on the screen. I forgot to hit save.

I do it now and wander to the back door while I open the messaging app and a new thread. The blank screen taunts me and my fingers tap out restless nonsense, no actual words. I open the back door for inspiration. The moon greets me, high and clear in the sky, stars blinking around her.

Fuck it.

I delete the gibberish and go with the truth.

Remy: *Moon-gazing and thinking of you.*

I'm not expecting a reply. He's already told me that night shifts involve the shouts from Hell or trying to catch some sleep on the reclining chairs that were swapped in for beds last year. Meaning, whatever he's doing, he's unlikely to have his phone in his hand.

I fire off the text and stuff the phone into my sleeping bag, irritated by how jittery I feel. It's been a long time—if ever— since anyone's got under my skin like Logan has. As much as I like him, I don't like *this*. Life has taught me not to depend on anyone, so why am I letting the skip in my heart keep me awake?

No clue. But keep me awake it does until it's time to roll down the hill to the post office.

The van protests, enjoying its rest at the top of the hill, and I'm glad Logan isn't home yet to hear the deep groan of the engine.

I ease the beast down the hill and into town. The post office is in the back of a corner shop. The kind that sells a million flavours of Monster, Pot Noodles, and not much else. But they have bacon. And eggs. After tapping my card for an eye-watering amount in postage, I buy food I have no facilities to cook.

In my defence, it's not for me.

I drive home sipping dirty Monster from the can. I'm not sleepy, but it's past time for that now anyway. I have more work to do.

It's still raining. I steer the van to the foot of Firefly Hill. The road is muddy and potholed. It takes all my concentration not to slide sideways, and by the time I reach Logan's house, I realise I'm not making it much further.

I'm not as upset about that as I might've been. The reason for that is the aged Land Rover Discovery on the driveway and the hunk of muscle hauling himself out.

I wonder how long he's been sitting there. I didn't see him on the road. Then I notice the phone pressed to his ear and it makes sense.

He doesn't see me straight away, too caught up in a call that's making him sigh and scrub a hand down his face.

I hop down from the van. The impact of my boots hitting the ground doesn't hurt and it's almost as good as seeing him.

Then Logan spots me and grins and nothing comes close.

He waves.

I wave back and grab the bag I brought back from the post office.

He points to his front door and mouths, "Come in?"

All right then.

I follow him inside, kicking my boots off at the door.

He's wearing *those* faded jeans and a tee I've seen before, long sleeves shoved up his forearms. No jacket, but after spending the night curled into his warm body, that worries me less.

We go to the kitchen. It's exactly as we left it yesterday. A couple of mugs in the sink. Crumbs on the chopping board from the toasties he made us before we left for the night.

Logan isn't saying much. Sounds like he's getting a coating from his ex, so I stay quiet and slip around him to set my bag on the counter.

He peers over my shoulder, body heat radiating. It's all I can do not sink back into him. I unpack instead and I know the minute he sees the bacon. His hand comes to my hip and he kisses my neck.

His lips linger before he straightens, hand sliding from my waist. "I said I'd do it, Bec. You don't need to bend my ear every fucking day."

Pause.

Then he sighs. "I'm not snapping. You're hounding me when I'm on nights. Leave me alone."

He speaks without aggression, but I can tell he's done. The call ends and he tosses the phone onto the counter, dropping his head to my neck again.

I reach back and slide my fingers into his hair. "All right?"

Logan hums, not moving, just leaning into me as if he *needs* me.

I like that feeling—not that he's vulnerable, but that he believes I'm strong enough to hold him up.

It's been a while since I last believed it.

I do now, though. I'll stand here all day if he wants me to.

He doesn't. A minute or so later, he tears himself away. "What are you doing with all that lovely food?"

"Making you breakfast."

"You mean *us*, right?"

"If you want company. Thought you might go straight to bed."

"Nah, I'm not there yet. I need a shower, though. You'll be all right a few minutes?"

I wave him away. I'm not much of a cook, but I can make breakfast baps without burning his house down.

Until he incinerates me a little while later when he comes back shirtless, old joggers sitting low on his hips.

Fucking hell. I saw him naked yesterday. I took a shower with him. Slid my dick between his lips while he knelt in front of me, and I survived. How's it possible that he's killing me stone dead from the other side of the room?

I turn the stove off. I've fried bacon and eggs, and slathered big white rolls with butter from his fridge.

He likes HP sauce. I hold out the bottle with his plate and he advances on me.

Our fingers brush. It does something to me I can't explain and I suck in a shaky breath that makes him frown.

"You okay?"

"Yup."

"Did you sleep last night?"

"Did you?"

He shrugs, barely blinking at the deflection. "A bit. Then we had to dig a lorry out of a ditch. Some of the boys are still there. What kept you up?"

You. "Work. I got some new orders and I was awake anyway. You wanna sit?"

Logan's a man who can inhale his breakfast twice over before it occurs to him to sit down. But he's not thinking about himself, he's thinking about me, and we decamp to the table.

He wants to know what I made while he was out there being a literal superhero.

I show him, appreciating his fascination more than I should. What I do is simple, it's just not many people think of it. What he does, on top of parenting *twins*?

There's no comparison.

Logan finishes his breakfast in four bites and keeps swiping through the photos on my phone.

My life is so uninteresting that I don't think to stop him. It dawns on me too late that's he's migrated out of jewellery town and into a life I've left behind.

"Is this Greenfest?"

"Isle of Wight. A few weeks later."

He's not looking at me, so he doesn't see me wince. Doesn't see me hide from the last moments I was the person he met last summer.

I rise and take the plates to the sink. My breakfast is half-eaten, but I'm done. I wrap it up and stash it in Logan's fridge. Maybe he can eat it later. When he wakes up to go and work all night again.

You should go.

"Remy."

Logan feels close, and his voice is so deep and low it's as good as him wrapping his big arms around me.

In reality, he hasn't moved. He's still at the table, holding my phone.

His searching gaze takes me prisoner. Latching on to the parts of me that want to run a mile. Not from him, but from how everything, all of it, makes me feel.

My feet become rooted to his kitchen floor. Logan puts my phone down, saying nothing, but his eyes are so expressive he doesn't need to. I hear what he's saying anyway.

Take a breath. When you're ready, come to me.

It doesn't take long. I'm not a wallower and he's magnetic enough that he could pull me out of a legitimate black hole.

I reclaim my seat.

Logan swivels his to face me and brushes my messy hair from my cheek. "What happened after?"

After I fell. I'm guessing he doesn't mean literally, and I'm glad about that. I've buried the bits I remember. "I was already living in my van for festival season. Getting banged up didn't change that. Only difference was I was alone, and I had no way of earning money when I couldn't honour my fire gigs."

"What about your jewellery business?"

"I couldn't move my hand for eight weeks. Or drive to get back to the workshop I was renting. I lost that too, and half the tools I had stored there."

Logan's face darkens. "Who stole your tools?"

I raise a hand to placate him, though angry Papa bear is a vibe I can appreciate. "No one. I was MIA for three months. By the time I got my shit together, the landlord had sold up and moved to Benidorm. My stuff got binned by the developers who bought the land."

Logan simmers down a little. "That sucks elephant balls."

I shrug. "Is what it is. I kept my Etsy store open and sold some pieces using the stuff I had stored in the van. Then I came here and your uncle gave me a chance, so it's not all bad."

"What would you have done if he hadn't?"

I frown into a grimace. "I don't know. I don't know if I want to perform again, so I might've gone home to my mum."

"Bingo lady in Port Talbot?"

"That's the one." I rub my shoulder. It doesn't hurt. Rarely does when I'm around Logan. But there's a wound in me that feels ripped open. I don't want to talk about myself anymore. "What about your parents?"

Logan props an elbow on the table and cradles his head in his hand. "Both dead. My ma passed when I was twenty-one. My dad a few years ago."

"I'm sorry."

"It's okay. I miss my mum. She'd have been the best grandma. But my dad...we weren't close. He drank a lot. Hated the fact that me and Locke were more sexually flexible than his old-fashioned soul was comfortable with. He wasn't proud of us and we weren't proud of him."

"Your brother's bisexual too?"

Logan grins. "Locke's probably more pan. He's doing the single dad thing at the moment too, but there's not much he's not down for."

"What about you?"

"You're asking about my sexuality now? After I've had your dick in my mouth?"

I love his bluntness. The way his rumbly voice wraps around filthy things. "I'm curious, not questioning. I've only ever been with dudes, but I'd be with a woman if I met someone who made me feel like I wanted to."

"How does that feel?" Logan edges a little closer. "Like this?"

He reaches for my hand and rubs his thumb over the pulse point in my wrist. It's a simple touch, but I shiver, goosebumps breaking over my skin. I want to tell him that no one, man or woman, has ever provoked a reaction like that before. But I settle for rolling my eyes. "Maybe."

Logan chuckles and lets me go. "I thought I was gay when I was younger. I didn't notice girls. Then we joined the fire service and being in that environment—where everything was so aggressively hetero...I don't know. I did what everyone else around me was doing and I didn't hate it. Then I met Bec and I loved her for a while, but when we split, my brain became dude-centric again and it felt right."

"It was Bec on the phone when you came home?"

Logan nods. "The farm projects. She's still worried I'm going to fuck it up."

"When are they due?"

"Next Friday."

"What have you got so far?"

Logan's eyes dim again. "Fuck all. I'll get to it. It's just... sometimes, the more she gets at me, the less capable I become, you know?"

I don't know. I have no clue what it's like to live Logan's life. Just that it's a lot, and he deserves more than the guilt weighing him down right now. "I can help. Making something out of nothing is my one skill."

Logan snorts. "Even if that's true, it's a pretty broad skill. Nothing singular about it."

I can't tell if he's being dirty. The sudden, deeper pulse in my blood says he is, but for once, his animated gaze gives nothing away. "Whatever. Bring the boys up when they come back and I'll see what I've got in the van."

"You don't have to do that."

"You don't have to not tell your uncle I'm using his workshop as a bunk house."

"He probably wouldn't care."

"Why haven't you told him then?"

Logan purses his lips. "I don't talk to him much."

"Fair enough." I push my chair back and stand. "I don't use half the crap I've been carting around my whole life. Maybe there's a compromise in there somewhere, eh?"

Logan rises too. He towers over me, but not on purpose. He's just really fucking big. "Maybe. You're leaving?"

"You need to sleep."

Logan swipes that devilish thumb under my left eye. "So do you."

"Not happening if I get back in your bed."

"You slept fine yesterday."

"How'd you know?"

"Cos I watched you."

Okay. That's my point in reverse. That if we fall into his bed, aside from all the shit that'll happen before we sleep, it's not the kind of rest he needs.

I should leave.

Before I never do.

I try to pull back, but he holds me firm, big hands clutching my wrists.

"Please? Stay for a bit? I won't jump you, I promise."

I let him tug me into his arms. He kisses me, which does nothing to convince me we won't end up naked the second we reach his bedroom, if not before.

No one has ever kissed me as much as he does. It's a whole body experience. A soul-shifting ride. I keep my eyes open so I don't float away, but I'm powerless to the weightless warmth he gifts me.

Only a glimpse of yet *another* box of Christmas decs keeps me bound to earth.

I nip Logan's bottom lip and pull away. "Was that here yesterday?"

Logan spares a glance over his shoulder. The box is tucked behind the kitchen door. "It's been there four months."

"Why?"

"These bouts of trying to be a good Christmas dad started early. Locke found that in our old bungalow. Don't even know what's in it."

"Could be crown jewels."

"Could be a pile of shit."

I don't ask him which is more likely—I think I already know. But I do lose the flicker of good intention I had six seconds ago.

I'm not leaving him.

Not yet.

I take his hand and pull him towards the stairs. "I'll stay till you're asleep. But no nakedness."

It seems a fair deal. Logan doesn't argue. He strips me to the cotton trousers I've been wearing all night and leaves his sweats on. We don't kiss again, both knowing where it leads, and crawl into his bed.

Logan stretches out on his side, head pillowed on his arm,

watching me. The shadow on his jaw looks a week old, dark and sexy.

I scratch my fingers over it.

He sighs and closes his eyes.

Moments later, he fades out, and I have every intention of going home.

Genius that I am, I fall asleep instead.

Logan

"You're totally banging him."

I fire Galen a glare over the top of the iPad screen that's currently filled with my brother's smug face. Locke and Galen don't know each other as well as they know me, but *Christ*, they're basically the same person.

Course they are. You miss your bro so much you found a BFF who's just like him.

Makes sense.

What doesn't is the fact they're both convinced I'm sleeping with Remy when I'm not. Sexually, at least. I slept all day with him.

I think.

He was gone when I woke up, and the catch on the landing window was no longer broken.

I point at Galen. "Shut the fuck up."

To my brother, I say, "I'm not banging anyone. Do I look that happy?"

Locke regards me. Even through FaceTime, eyes that are mine pierce my soul. "You look something," he says eventually. "Like you don't have a broom handle up your—"

"All right." I interrupt. "Fuck off if that's all you called to talk about."

"I didn't call to talk about anything. Just miss your face."

"Look in the mirror then."

"Aw, fuck-a-duck, Lo. Everyone knows you're the pretty one."

Not true. I'm just tidier than my biker brother. Because I have to be. Breathing apparatus and helmets don't fit around the mess on his jaw and the shaggy blond mop on his head. I have structure and rules in my life where he has none.

He chose that, remember? Stop acting like it's a Greek tragedy.

Fuck it. "I miss you too."

Galen takes his cue and disappears.

The rest of the conversation skirts around the fact that Locke senses something is up in my life. His kids are in the background. Teenagers, all attitude and insecurities. Locke's a good dad, but those kids are feral.

When he's gone, I wonder if I should do more to help him with that, but a shout comes in before I can dwell on it too much, and it's morning before I know it.

I drive home dreaming about spending the day with Remy in my bed. But he's not around. Firefly Hill is devoid of the smoke coming from the workshop chimney and his van is gone.

He left. My pulse nosedives. I grip the steering wheel a little too hard and it creaks under the pressure before I get a handle on myself. *Calm your tits. He has errands to run, just like everyone else.*

Remy is nothing like everyone else. But the logic steadies me enough to park my car and go inside.

My house feels empty. And cold. I hate wasting gas when I'm alone, but the boys will be home tonight, so I crank the heating and take a shower.

Then, because I know I can't handle my kids without a nanna nap under my belt, I pass out on the couch.

As usual, I wake with minutes to spare before I have to leave for school pick-up. I've done no washing. My clothes are scattered around the house, none of them clean. I gather some up and shove them in the machine, tug on the same shit I came home in, and hightail it out of the door.

It's food shop day. I should've gone before I picked up the boys, but I'm an idiot, so I have to burn around Tesco with them hanging off me.

Fuck my life. I love my kids, but it takes every ounce of restraint not to leave them in the meat aisle.

Back home, I sling too many frozen pizzas in the oven and help them with their homework. Discover a damp load of washing in the dryer that smells like the devil's swamp.

I'm losing my shit in the utility room when Billy comes to tell me there's someone at the door.

"Who?" I snap.

"Dunno. Didn't open it, did I?"

Course he didn't. He's not allowed. But he could've at least peeked through the window, right? Because if it's anyone except Remy, I'm not fucking answering it.

It is Remy. He's got a dark wool hat shoved over his hair and two big IKEA bags at his feet. "I found some stuff. For the farms."

It takes me a second to compute the context. Mainly because I'm struck dumb by how fucking beautiful he is. It's sleeting outside, and there are literal tiny snowflakes on his lashes. Christ on a cracker, I'm in trouble.

Breath caught, I wave him inside.

He slips by, pausing right in front of me. "All right?"

I nod. *Keep walking, dear God. Before I do something crazy.*

Remy ventures further into the house.

Sam comes running and hugs his legs. Another sign that this enchanting dude is worth more than anything I've given him so far.

My shy kid doesn't hug anyone except me, Locke, and his ma.

Billy doesn't hug much because he's rarely still for that long, but he appears from the living room too, face brightening as his gaze lands on Remy. "It was you at the door."

"It was," Remy agrees. "Maybe we should have a special knock so you know it's me."

"Without looking?"

"Yeah."

Billy is fascinated and I lose Remy to them figuring out a rhythm that's going to drive me up the wall when Remy's gone and Billy's banging it out on every available surface.

Sam's less attracted to making noise for no reason. He spies Remy's bags and peeks inside. I don't stop him cos I know Remy won't. "Dad, what are these?"

I glance through the kitchen door. "Pipe cleaners."

"What are they for?"

"Clue's in the name, bud. What words did I say?"

Sam frowns and turns his back on me.

Remy's chuckle finds me from the depths of the living room and he rescues Sam from his wondering. "They're fuzzy wires to clean old man pipes with. Bendy, so they go round corners. I thought you could make people out of them for your model farm."

Sam's frown melts and his little face lights up enough that I have to back away, unable to watch as Remy unloads his magic bag onto the living room rug.

I retreat to the kitchen, sucking in a deep breath that goes nowhere. I don't feel bad that Remy's better at this than I am. That it was him who put that smile on my son's face instead of me. Instead, I feel connected to something I'm not sure is permanent, and it scares me to death.

Don't let them get close to him. What if he doesn't want anything serious? Fuck, what if he leaves?

Damn. Until those thoughts blistered into my brain, I hadn't been thinking of anything serious either, but as my kids' soft laughter filters into the kitchen, my heart does a flip it's not going to recover from.

I like this dude.

I like *Remy*.

Fuck, I like him a lot.

I drift back to the utility room and stuff stinky towels into the washing machine for another cycle. Possibly their third, can't remember. I wash my hands, then put another wet load into the dryer absolutely certain I won't forget about it.

It's an optimistic state of mind.

Misguided, most likely. But I don't give a fuck about the washing. Everything I care about is in my living room.

The oven timer beeps.

I go back to the kitchen and ponder if my heart knew Remy would be here tonight. There's enough pizza, garlic bread, and coleslaw for a thousand people.

Or, you know, four.

I poke my head in the living room. No one looks up, too busy rummaging through Remy's bags.

Billy is hanging over Remy's shoulder, arms around his neck. "Can I make a dinosaur farm?"

"Ask your dad." Remy checks in on Sam, who's so close he might as well be on his lap. "You want to make fence from lollipop sticks? I have loads, look. We can paint them."

Yup. Still not ready for this scene. But I can't bring myself to break it up, either. I bring the dinner into the living room and set it on the coffee table. "Come eat, all of you."

The boys reluctantly get up.

Remy stays put. "You don't have to feed me."

"You don't have to spend your evening on my living room floor, either."

"No?" He shoots me a filthy smirk.

I roll my eyes. "Humour me."

"Yes, Papa."

This. Dude.

Remy unfolds his long body from the carpet and joins me on the sofa. He sits close, but we're not touching, and it makes my skin itch with how much I wish we were.

I eat mechanically, pushing more food on Remy until he begs me to stop.

"You're a feeder," he accuses.

"He wants you to get hairs on your chest," Billy pipes up. "It's why we eat vegetables."

I choke on my beer. How does every piece of parent crap that comes out of my mouth come back to haunt me in the end?

Also, Remy already has hair on his chest. Less than me, but it's dark and soft and I want to bury my face in it.

I wash the plates with a fucking semi.

Remy goes back to helping the kids choose the bits they want to use for their farms. By the time I'm composed enough to join them, he's leaving.

I want him to stay.

I know he can't. Not with the kids here.

Not yet. Maybe not ever.

It's a horrible thought.

Remy spots my frown and backs me into the kitchen, taking my hands in his. "What's wrong?"

"Nothing."

He cocks a brow, waiting. But I can't tell him the madness dancing through my brain. Can't find the fucking words.

"I don't want you to go," I say, because it's true.

Remy's expression softens. "I'll be back."

"When?"

"Whenever you want me. You have my number now, right?"

I do. I never got round to answering his text the other day because Bec derailed me, but the simple words he sent...can't count how many times I've read them. "I'm off for the next few days. I'll find you?"

Remy smiles. "You will. Goodnight, Papa."

He kisses the tip of my nose.

Then he's gone.

He's right, naturally. Every time I come out of my house, Remy is outside the workshop.

I tempt him down the hill every night for the next three days. He spends his evenings on the floor with the boys, building farms out of things I never thought of. I feed him my mediocre cooking while he crafts animals and buildings from sticks and paper.

Billy gets his dinosaur farm. There's a T-rex made from a loo roll and scraps of old leather, and some kind of therapod bird thing with pigeon feathers sprayed green.

It's grotesque and brilliant.

Sam's farm is small and intricate. They're still working on it when Bec arrives to pick them up, and it dawns on me I haven't told her about Remy.

That I should've.

I've never had anyone around the boys before. But as she eases her car through the fixed gate, it's too late to pull Sam from Remy's lap.

I leave him there and hold my breath.

Bec breezes into my house. Her gaze sweeps the living space before it lands on me and she points at the kitchen.

Shit.

I shut the door behind me.

Bracing myself.

My ex-wife...*grins*.

"So that's the hottie from up the hill, eh?"

"What?"

Bec laughs. "Relax. I saw the boys at school today, remember? It was my turn to help at reading club."

I don't remember. Not at all. "What's that got to do with Remy?"

"Uh, I don't know. Maybe that the boys won't shut up about him and Sam saw you kissing him on the driveway last night?"

Oh. I remember doing that. As the days have passed, it's become harder and harder to let Remy go every night. I want him in my bed. I've only slept with him twice, but without him, my sheets feel cold and rough against my skin. Most nights I've given up and crashed on the couch.

"It's okay, Lo," Bec says when I fail to formulate a response. "You're allowed to have a life. And Christ, I know you wouldn't have anyone dodgy around the boys. I trust you."

My brows shoot into my hairline. "You do?"

Bec smacks my arm. "Of course. I only get on your case about the stuff you don't care about."

Not caring has never been the problem and she knows it. But I'm not about to start a fight when she's on my side for the first time in forever.

She rounds up the boys.

Remy loads the finished farms into her car boot and disappears.

When the boys are gone, I feel so fucking bereft it chokes me.

Then slender, tattooed arms wind around me from behind. Remy presses cool lips to my neck. "How long you got, Papa?"

I lean back into him, tension leaving my body. "Till when?"

"Till you have to leave for work."

My shift pattern is on its head this week. Norovirus and

holidays have fucked everything up. I'm heading into three consecutive nights. "I've got an hour."

Remy turns me round. His coffee bean eyes are alight with mischief and heat. "That'll do."

I let him lead me inside. We don't make it to my bed. He blows me on the couch as I tangle my fingers in his messy hair and growl swear words at the ceiling.

This...the physical part. It's easy. I could fool around with him forever.

But it's the *forever* part that spins me. I have no idea where Remy's head is at. If the future is even on his radar.

All I know is that I want it.

Remy

Logan's run of night shifts seems to last forever. I fall into a pattern of working all night and waiting up for him to come home.

I make him breakfast. Shower with him and curl up with him in his bed, knowing I'll wake some time later to him doing wild things to my body.

Logan is a selfless lover. He likes me sucking his dick, but he spends far more time sucking mine, turning me inside out until I come so hard I'm scared I'll have a fucking stroke.

He doesn't try to bang me, though. Not with his cock. He gives me earth-shattering orgasms with lubed fingers, and his hot tongue, then eases me onto my back so he can come on my chest.

It's hot as hell, but the sensation that he's holding back is hard to ignore.

He works a day shift when the boys are due home. I keep watch for his car coming back after school pick-up, but it doesn't happen.

An hour after he's due, his ex-wife shows up instead.

I'm in Logan's house, by accident. I need the pliers I left in his kitchen and I'm exiting the front door as the boys tumble out of their mum's car.

"Remy!" Tiny arms and legs bundle into me.

I hug them back, then retreat, unsure of how their mum will feel about them climbing all over me.

She's more chill than I expect. "It's okay. I know they all love you."

All? I blink.

Bec shuts her car door and sends the boys inside. "Logan's late," she tells me. "Did he call you?"

"Me? No."

"Oh. Well, he's caught up in something. I don't know when he'll be back, the station manager didn't know."

I don't know why she's telling me this. Or why she's here. Just that whatever's making Logan late for his boys isn't anything pleasant. "Okay. You need my help with something?"

Bec eyes me, conflict raging in a gaze that would probably be pretty if I wasn't bewitched by her ex-husband. "I'm supposed to go to Bristol tonight. I have an art exhibition opening tomorrow, at the Red Lodge Museum."

"That's cool."

"Won't be if I'm not there. How serious are you about Logan?"

"Excuse me?"

Bec steps closer. "He's serious about you. He won't say it to me, but there's no way you'd be as close to this house and our boys if he wasn't."

I know that already. The way Logan looks at me sometimes before he catches himself, it's...intense. And I feel that. I'm obsessed with him. Sometimes I think I might love him, but that's ridiculous, right? We've only known each other a month or so.

We haven't even fucked—*like that's what matters?*

Besides, whether he knows it or not, Logan kept me

company the entire time I was laid up and broken in hospital. When I was crying into the cold in the back of my van. That god-like man from the summer...fuck, my imagination of him then had nothing on what he's actually like.

He's so sweet. So kind.

So funny without trying.

Without *knowing* half the time.

Am I serious about him?

About his gorgeous boys?

Yeah. I think I am. But I'm not about to spill my heart to his ex-wife before I get around to spilling it to him.

I speak plainly. "What do you need from me, Bec? You need me to watch the boys until Logan gets home? Cos that feels like something he should have a say in."

"He's not here."

"So?"

"So..." Bec drags her gaze between me and front door. "That's something you should get used to. There's always going to be something more important than you. Than all of us. I hear what you're saying, though, and if you're not comfortable doing it, I'll take them to my mum's, but they'd rather be here with you. They told me that the second they found out Lo was stuck at work."

I don't know her well enough to trust she's speaking the truth and not using my obvious affection for her boys to get her own way. But I do know this: she's not evil. She's just a woman trying to live her life on top of parenting two tiny humans.

Logan's tiny humans. "All right. I'll stay with them. But I'm gonna tell you I think it's fucking weird that you trust me with your kids when you don't even know me."

Bec grins a little and pats my arm. "You're right, I don't know you. But I know Logan, and there's no way you'd be here if you weren't the best bloke he'd ever met."

It's quite the compliment. But I still think the whole thing is strange. I think *she's* strange and I tell Logan so in a text message that's probably the last thing he needs to read when he gets back to the station from wherever he is.

Remy: *Your weirdo ex-wife left the boys with me. We're going to eat baked beans and play* Minecraft. *They're safe, I promise. Sam just asked me to cut his hair, tho…*

I don't cut Sam's hair. I feed him and his brother beans on toast, and we play computer games until my eyes feel square.

Fuck this.

I drag the box of decorations from behind the kitchen door. We dig through it and find solar lights. "Kids, get your shoes on."

They think I'm loopy. Maybe I am, but we have more fun hooking the lights around the crooked tree at the end of the driveway then we ever will inside.

The lights are dim. "They'll be brighter tomorrow, after a day in the sun."

The boys don't care. They're cold and dirty and happy, and that's enough for them.

We head back inside.

I find hot chocolate in the cupboard and load them with sugar before sending them to find pyjamas.

I'm staring, bemused, at the result when headlights sweep the ground floor of Logan's cosy house.

He's home.

I'm nervous. I don't know why—he replied to my garbled message an hour ago.

With a green love heart.

Oh man.

His car crawls into its usual spot. The engine shuts off and the lights die. I move to the window, watching in the darkness as he pauses before he gets out, scrubbing two hands down a face bathed in shadow.

He's tired. Of course he is. This shift was overtime. But it feels like more than that. Logan exits his car on legs that seem to move too slow. As if they're weighted with something I'll never understand.

His boys are still chasing each other round the sofa, dressed in what looks like reject PE kit and Halloween costumes. "Little dudes," I call. "Dad's home."

Then I get out of the way as Logan finally eases the front door open.

It's a while before I venture out of the kitchen. Logan's still in the hallway, sitting on the floor with Sam while Billy jumps around them.

He's holding Sam so fucking close, and he meets my gaze with bloodshot eyes.

I lean in the kitchen doorway. "All right?"

Logan takes a deep inhale of Sam's tousled hair. "Am now."

I leave it at that and retreat to the kitchen again. Maybe I should leave. But I don't. I wash dishes and boil the kettle.

I'm stirring milk into tea when I feel him behind me, his broad body dwarfing mine, his chin on my shoulder.

"It makes a difference," he says quietly. "Not coming home to an empty house. Thank you."

I reach back and take his hand. "Wouldn't be anywhere else, Papa."

A low sound mumbles from him. It's a moment where his lips usually touch my neck, but this hits different. He doesn't kiss me. He sighs from deep in his soul, and returns to his boys.

I still don't leave.

Sam calls me into the living room. We watch Marvel movies until midnight while Logan swings between dragging his kids into bear hugs and staring into space.

Sometime around one, he carries them to bed, beckoning for me to follow him upstairs.

There's still a part of me that wants to leave. *No.* Want isn't the right word. And I don't know what is. But trailing Logan up the stairs tonight feels loaded. A path that can't be untrodden.

He disappears with the boys.

I slip into the bathroom, taking a moment of groundless solitude. I can hide from this as much as I like. I'm still not fucking leaving.

After splashing water on my hot face, I step onto the landing.

Logan is at the window, gazing out into the night. "That tree looks amazing."

"You like it?"

"Almost as much as the boys like you."

I snort. "It's easy to be the fun babysitter."

"It's more than that, Rem."

Tightness locks my throat. I step forward in the same moment Logan turns. The landing is dark, the only sliver of light from the half-hidden moon. Logan shivers, and I close the distance between us in a thud of my restless heart.

He threads his arms around me.

I hook mine around his neck. "What do you need?"

He answers my whisper with a kiss that's as gentle as it is demanding, simmering with a desire that makes him shake, the tremor in his big, strong arms a reminder, as if I need one, that he's not the same man he was when he kissed me yesterday.

The kiss goes on and on. I don't realise we're moving until the faint light from the window disappears.

His bedroom smells familiar—cotton sheets and man.

The intensity of his hold on me is new, but I know how it's gonna end.

We fall onto the bed. Logan strips our clothes and rolls us under the covers, for my benefit, not his. Though for once, I'm not cold. There's no time, not when he's seeping heat and sex into me with every touch.

He's so hard, everywhere from his cut chest to his thick

cock. What he wants to do with it should scare me, but I want it.

I want *him*.

"Remy." Logan murmurs my name against my lips, more heat bubbling over, air vacuumed from my lungs.

He feels so good against me. Whatever he's about to ask of me, with or without words, the answer is yes.

Fuck, it's a thousand times yes.

Logan pulls me harder against him, flesh colliding in a deeper grind. His heartbeat thumps against my chest in perfect synchrony with my own thundering pulse. He ransacks every desire we've vaulted over the past few months, or however long it's truly been. I feel him in ways I've never felt anyone, and it's me who reaches for the drawer in his bedside table.

His sinful stash is right at the back, hidden in a sock. It's a moment of levity, but our shared grin is swallowed by the untamed current thrumming between us.

Logan kisses me with a force that electrifies my nerves. He lays me down and plays my body with his fingers and tongue until I'm a sweaty, shuddering mess, every groan swallowed down by my forearm jammed over my mouth.

I catch his wrist in my slippery grasp. "Now," I whisper. "Whatever you want, do it now."

"What do *you* want?" He stares so fucking deep, as if whatever I say isn't enough to convince him I want this too.

I pull him over me, hooking my legs over his. "Fuck me."

My words are barely audible, but I see every syllable hit him. See his gaze darken and his pupils expand. His teeth dig into his bottom lip.

He reaches for a condom and rolls one onto his dick. He's big. I knew it already. But I'm not worried about him hurting me. His tongue is so wicked the only pain I'm gonna feel is the unsated *ache* if this doesn't happen.

Logan lubes up and pulls my leg to his chest, big hand

resting on my knee. He breaks our stare a moment to line us up. Then his gaze pins me down, hot and unwavering, as he slowly sinks inside me.

Holy fucking—shit fuck.

A groan wedges in my throat, instant and rough. I swallow it down, screwing my eyes shut, earth-shattering sensation blistering into me.

Goddamn.

My legs tremble.

I'm already clenching around him, this *fear* he'll pull out all-consuming.

He doesn't pull out. Face taut with strain, he keeps pushing, deeper and harder, until he's buried to the hilt and kissing me, smothering the sounds I can't.

Logan fucks me with steady thrusts that turn my soul inside out, rolling me onto my belly, moulding his whole body around mine.

It's...fuckingfuck. I can't. It's too good. My breaths shudder from my lungs in snatched, hot gasps, and I force his hand over my mouth, as if I can shove the noise back inside.

Above me, Logan grunts, snapping his hips harder, bracing himself on the edge of the bed I'm hanging off. "I'm gonna come so hard inside you."

I believe his harsh whisper. It's in every brutal drive of his cock, every strangled, suppressed sound he makes. And I need it to happen. Before I explode into a million pieces and I'm never whole again.

The pleasured coil in my belly starts to unravel. My dick is trapped beneath me, pressed to the mattress by Logan's weight, at the mercy of the friction there. Overcome, I sink my teeth into Logan's palm, arching my back.

And we come hard together in total silence.

Logan

I had sex with Remy.

The thought plays on repeat the moment I open my eyes, alarm blaring, catapulting me from sleep.

It's so sudden, so vivid, I almost bolt upright, but my arms are full. As being awake settles in my bones, I stay where I am, silencing the alarm with a clumsy hand.

A mess of LEGO pieces fall to the floor. Not that many, and it's not that loud, but Remy jumps, and I whisper an apology to his temple. "Shh, I'm sorry. Go back to sleep."

He murmurs something, but turns into my chest, his words muffled. I have no idea what he said. Just that he's here, in my bed, as naked as when we passed out together, sweat barely cooled on our skin.

I am *so* tired. That deep-rooted fatigue that brings nausea and grit to my eyes. I tighten my arms around Remy and bury my face in his hair. But I can't go back to sleep. *The boys.* It's early. They won't be up for a while yet. But they can't find Remy naked in my bed.

Honestly, they can't find anyone naked in my bed.

I cling to Remy a moment longer, then kiss him again before easing out of bed.

It's fucking *cold*.

I stumble to the thermostat, collecting clothes on the way, and poke at it until I hear the boiler spark to life. Then I force myself into the shower, keeping a sharp ear out for the creak of the boys' door.

For once, God is on my side. I don't hear a peep out of them until I'm clean, dressed, and my bedroom door is closed.

I guide a sleepy Sam right past it and haul Billy out of his pit. We barely make it downstairs before Sam lets me know I've wasted my energy.

"Are you going to take Remy a cup of tea?"

"Hmm?" I fumble with the kettle and slide my gaze to the window and Remy's empty workshop. "Uh. He's probably not up yet. There's no lights on, see?"

"Because he's upstairs, silly." Sam blinks his huge eyes at me, looking so much like my brother that for a moment I think he's taking the piss. But not this kid, man. He's my angel boy, and he has me so fucking rumbled I can only stare at him. "Err..."

"He doesn't really like tea," Billy pipes up. "Make him coffee instead."

Fucking hell.

How do they know that and I don't?

Because they just spent an entire evening with him that's probably shifted your friendship more than fucking him in your bed.

Wow. Really?

But the more I think about it, the more real it becomes. Us having sex has been on the table a while now. Remy being my ex's go-to babysitter is something I didn't see coming, and now my mind is less hazy from the shift from hell, I can see how skewed it is.

Bec trusted Remy because she knows we're...something, and she trusts *me*. But Remy didn't know that, so how the hell did that seem from his point of view? My ex dumping my kids on him?

Christ, what if he thinks it was my idea? That I fast-tracked him to step-parenting before we'd even fucked. Goddamn, without *asking* him if, light years in the future, it's a role he'd ever want?

The sliver of reason I have left knows this man has a pure fucking heart. That he'd never get as close to my boys as he has if he didn't give a shit. But caring doesn't mean permanence, and being scared to death of that fact stops me from registering that I haven't questioned how *I* feel.

That it's only Remy who matters because my mind is already made up.

It hits me again.

The future. I want it.

And Christ, if I learned anything yesterday, it was that life's too short to wait for it to happen.

"Dad, you're pouring milk everywhere."

Fuck's sake. Ignoring Billy's amusement, I mop up the mess I've made and mix up two mugs of instant coffee. "Does he have sugar? I can't remember."

Billy shoves a Nutri-Grain bar in his mouth, dropping crumbs into a mug I suppose is now mine. "Dunno."

I should know. I've made Remy coffee before...I think. But my brain is a strange place on the back of a tough shift. Small things escape me, like I'm flailing underwater while the rest of the world goes on without me.

Remy pulls me over him, hooking his legs over mine. "Fuck me."

All right. So I remember that part. The heady, *whispered* part as we had bone-shaking, silent sex.

Priorities.

I pry the box of cereal bars from Billy's sticky hands and

pass one to Sam. "Eat these and go watch TV, okay? I'll bring your uniforms down."

As if they don't already know Remy's in my bed. But the change in our usual routine is a fun one. They don't question it and I watch them bounce off to the couch before scooping up the mug without crumbs floating in it and heading for the stairs.

My bedroom door is still closed. I bypass it for a moment and rummage clean school uniforms from the chest in the boys' room.

I make a pile on the top step, then give into the deep yearning in my gut and slip into my room.

My gaze falls on Remy and the agitation I've ruminated myself into fades. It doesn't evaporate completely, but the sight of him sleeping in my sex rumpled sheets hits me like a Valium.

I exhale a long, slow breath and round the bed to where Remy is on his side, facing the window. There's a tiny ray of morning light filtering through a gap in the curtains. It hits his sunshine hair just right and another wave of calm washes over me.

It's so easy to brush a stray lock from his face. So right. I don't want to disturb him, but there's a compulsion in me to keep touching and touching and touching him until he wakes up.

He keeps me waiting for three heavy thuds of my heart. Then his breathing changes and his brown eyes flutter open. There's a beat where he doesn't remember where he is or what we've done. I see it in the haze that passes through his lovely face.

Then he smiles, slow and soft, and I know, for now at least, that everything's okay.

Remy rolls onto his back and stretches. The duvet slides down, revealing his tattooed torso. "You all right, Papa?"

Christ, he's so beautiful it almost hurts to look at him. "Hmm?"

Remy rubs my thigh. "I wouldn't have minded if you'd hustled me out last night. If you didn't want the boys to see us."

"They already saw us. Well, Sam did. He told Bec we were, uh, kissing on the driveway."

"Oh." Remy blinks harder to wake himself up. Then studies my face. "How do you feel about that?"

"How do you feel about it?"

"Why does that matter?"

Because I need to know if it makes you happy or want to run a fucking mile. But I don't say that. I get tongue-tied and pass him the coffee instead. "I need to get the boys ready and take them to school. You hungry?"

Remy eyes me over the rim of his mug. The more he stares, the more my mind drifts to how I fucked him last night. How bad I *needed* to and how scared I was that he'd say no.

Irrationally scared. My soul knew he wasn't gonna. That he wanted me as much as I've always wanted him.

But to need someone like that...I can't explain it, and it makes me feel unhinged.

"Logan." Remy squeezes my leg. Waits for me to refocus before he speaks again. "Whatever's freaking you out, it's fine. You don't have to marry me just because we fucked. And you don't have to fuck me ever again if it's too messy for you."

"What?"

Remy smiles as though he's the one making sense. "It's okay. We're friends. Nothing else matters."

I'm too bamboozled to refute those statements. Especially as he's right. We are friends. And I'm grateful. But he's wrong about nothing else mattering. Everything and everyone, it all matters.

God, why can't I just say that without weighing him down with baggage he didn't order?

Your kids aren't baggage. I know that. But what about my job? It's already stealing his freedom and we're not even together.

Remy sets his mug down and rises up on his knees behind me, embracing me. "Stop thinking," he whispers. "I'm here for you whatever, okay?"

I don't want whatever. I want him. But I've run out of time to find my words. As reasonable as Bec was about me smooching Remy in front of the boys, being late for school is a cardinal sin.

Remy hops out of bed and starts to gather his clothes.

I stand. Reach for him as if that'll keep him naked in my bed forever. "I'm sorry."

"What for?"

"I don't know."

"Then don't be sorry." Remy grins and kisses my cheek. "It's not your fault life is complicated. Just breathe, yeah? The furthest I'm going is up the hill."

How he knew it was the thought of him leaving that was shaking me up, I have no idea. But it makes it easier to let him go.

I kiss his temple and shuffle back downstairs. The kids are in no mood to get ready for school, knowing Remy is upstairs. I'm irate by the time we leave, until I catch Remy's wink from the landing window.

He'll be gone by the time I get back, but his words sit with me. "*The furthest I'm going is up the hill.*" It's a weird feeling to know I'd probably cry if it wasn't.

It's healthy to be emotional after bad shifts. You'd be a robot if you weren't.

Sad, but true. But it's hard to think of the fuzz in my head and the itch in my skin as anything that's good for me.

Call your brother.

Best advice ever. Thanks, subconscious. Locke knows the job. And he knows me better than anyone.

Half an hour later, buoyed by my brother's patented pound shop wisdom, I'm in the supermarket, buying condoms, lube, and extra chicken for tonight's dinner.

Heh, maybe I'm just a closet optimist.

I drive home past the tree Remy and the boys decorated last night. In daylight, more strings of solar bulbs are visible, making me wonder how crazy it's going to look under the stars tonight. How much more I'm gonna love it. *Why did it never occur to me to put lights outside?*

Because I'm never around enough to do anything properly. An unfair assessment Bec would be proud of.

A fed up sigh gusts out of me. I reach the cottage, grab the shopping from the boot, and head into my empty house. It's my day off. There's shit everywhere that needs doing, but I don't care enough to do it. Instead, I drag the remaining boxes of Christmas decorations into the living room, and fetch a couple more from the loft.

I'm staring at them when I remember the boxes in the downstairs cloakroom.

I go to fetch them and heft them out. A sparkle catches my eye on the basin tap. A copper-coloured glittery bow. It makes no sense at all and I frown so hard my face aches.

Then I remember. It was dripping like a motherfucker and I stacked boxes in front of it to block it out of my life.

It's not dripping now.

And my dick is hard.

Wow.

It's quite the combination of circumstances, and I drift back to the living room in a daze. Meander to the kitchen. Open the fridge. Shut it again. The door doesn't hang like it used to, like it could crash to the ground at any moment. Someone's replaced the hinges, and it wasn't me.

Remy. There's no copper-coloured Christmas bow attached to the fridge, but there doesn't need to be for me to know it was him. That somewhere among the time he spent taking care of my children, or even in the time he's spent making me feel more human than I have in years, he's fixed the little things.

Little things that add up to a primal craving for him I can't ignore.

I spin away from the fridge and blow out of my house like a fucking whirlwind.

It's a small miracle I'm still wearing my boots, but I'm not convinced I'd have noticed the frosty ground beneath my socked feet if I hadn't been.

I jog up the hill, the steep incline nothing to legs that have charged up and down more flights of stairs and ladders than I'll ever be able to count.

The workshop doors are closed, but there's smoke blooming from the chimney. He's there. Even if logic didn't tell me so, I'd feel it in my bones.

I don't want him to have to stop what he's doing to hoist the rolling door. I duck round the back and let myself in.

As ever, his battered radio is tuned to the festive station. I brace myself for more Wham!, but it's Dean Martin this time and I can live with that.

Remy is standing over the sink, brushing his teeth. He's shirtless, taking advantage of the warmth kicking out from the loaded stove, dressed only in moss-green trousers and socks.

His back is so beautiful. My hands itch to touch him, but I'm not a dude who sneaks up on anyone. I clear my throat, letting him know I'm right fucking here.

Remy meets my gaze in the cracked mirror. He spits, then shuts his eyes with a shaky inhale. "Did you hear me thinking about you?"

"Maybe." I draw closer and mould my body to his, curving

around his elegant spine and kissing his neck. Biting a little. "I was thinking about you too."

"Oh yeah? What were you thinking?"

Lots of things, but now I have him in my arms again, my mind blanks. I run my palms over his bare skin, breathing him in, kissing along his jaw until I find his mouth and claim it.

It's not a gentle kiss. It's demanding and he lets me in, arching his neck, pressing back against me, a low moan breaching his lips.

Holy hell. This isn't what I came up here for, but sensation eviscerates my memory. I'm no longer stuffed full of things I need to say. I'm just a man who can't resist this magical fucking human.

It escalates fast—faster than it ever has when we've been naked. I'm so hard. And I need inside him. That we're rucked up against the sink in my uncle's workshop doesn't cross my mind.

I shove Remy's clothes aside and fumble with mine. The lube and condoms are in my pocket, in case I forgot to bring the shopping in from the car and the boys collected the bags instead. Have I been preparing for this moment my whole fucking life?

Remy watches me roll a condom on, his gaze hooded in the broken mirror. He's breathing hard, skin flushed from my rough hands.

"You need—?"

"No." He braces himself on the wall. "Just do it."

I lube up and align us. Despite his words, I ease in so fucking slowly my eyes roll and every nerve in my body protests.

Let 'em protest. I'm not hurting him. Not for anything. I wait for his body to relax, fighting baser instincts. It takes minutes, seconds, I have no idea. Just that it's a lifetime I'll endure a thousand times over to get to what comes next.

I curve around him again, reaching over his shoulders to

clasp my hands over his, supporting myself as much as him. I grind my hips in a slow circle, but it's not a pace I can sustain. A frantic need overcomes me. I fuck him hard. Fast and deep. My jeans slip down my thighs and my T-shirt bunches up. My abdomen slides against Remy's bare back, and it's everything.

We don't have to be quiet. And we're not. As Christmas crooners filter from the radio, moans and hitched breaths pitch low, a filthy soundtrack to our bodies colliding.

"Fuck." Remy staggers a little. "That's so fucking good."

It's better than good, but I'm out of adjectives, if I ever had many. I give myself up to the heat blistering through me, pressing my forehead to Remy's shoulder. A brutal climax detonates inside, but I fight it. *Him first.*

Somehow, I find the balance to drop a hand from the wall and wrap my fist around his dick. I squeeze him and he comes with a strangled sound, goosebumps littering his skin.

It's more than I can handle, the way his whole body shudders and clenches around me. I drive into him, over and over, chasing a peak.

When I reach it, I stay inside him, pressing deep, coming with a harsh and shattering groan.

I'm not built for orgasms like this. I don't know how I stay on my feet, let alone how I'll ever recover. Only the fear of letting Remy fall keeps me upright.

I hold him tight, absorbing a tremor I realise is laughter. "What's so funny?"

Remy bites the arm I've banded around his throat. "You are. I have every right to be surprised that you came up here and banged me against the wall. What's your excuse for looking so shocked?"

"I, uh, didn't know it would be that good?"

"Seriously?"

"No. I'm shocked that it happened. I didn't come up here for that. For *this*." I'm still inside Remy. I pull out, holding his hips steady, belatedly mindful he's still in recovery. "Shit. Did I hurt you?"

He laughs again. "Fuck, no. You think *anything* about that was bad?"

I don't think anything as I ditch the condom. Can't. My brain is in pieces. I pull my jeans back up and his sexy-as-fuck hippie trousers, and shake my head. "I'm a fucking mess."

"Welcome to the club." Remy eyes me a moment. Then drags his lips over my cheek. "Wanna help me with something?"

"Hmm?"

He holds out a hand. "Come with me, Papa."

Remy leads me to his workbench. On the surface are a thousand pennies and a cloth. He puts me to work, keeping my hands busy and quieting my noisy mind.

I'm supposed to polish the pennies till they shine. But a wise man once told my kids that nothing perfect ever looks that way.

They believed him.

So do I.

Remy

Logan wants to talk. But he doesn't know what he wants to say. Or how to say it. So he says nothing for days and days and days, and neither do I.

I watch him wrap presents and buy a ginormous turkey that he chucks in the freezer.

And we fuck a lot. Eat dinner together most nights he's home before he coaxes me to spend the night in his bed.

The sex is crazy. Logan has this way of fucking me. His whole body covers mine, his weight pressing me into the bed as he curls his hips, fucking me so deep I can't see how we'll ever be two separate people again.

I just need to come and survive it. It's my only endgame, even while my heart screams for something more.

"Shit, Remy." Logan winds his arm around my throat. *"I could fuck you forever."*

Forever.

It's not a word I've ever considered mine. I've never wanted it. But as Logan envelops me, consciously or not, with everything he has, it becomes a tick in my brain I can't ignore.

Fuck. I think I love him.

Nope. I *know* I do. And I think he might love me back. I just have to wait for him to catch up.

Is that where the forever part kicks in?

Logan has a big life—lots of moving parts and demands on his heart. Maybe there's no room for another one and loving him means letting him go.

Fuck that.

Whoa.

Okay.

I'm in his cottage when that thought kicks in, in the living room, listening to Billy try to persuade me that I can't really tell him and Sam apart.

"We look exactly the same," he insists.

"It's not about how you look." I mess his hair up. "It's how you hold yourself."

Billy frowns. "I don't hold myself. Dad told me not to."

I don't want to know what that conversation was about. I want Logan to come back from washing Blu Tack out of Sam's hair because I miss him. But I saw that wodge. He's gonna be a while.

"It's not literal." I fudge an explanation. "Your brother wouldn't stand in front of me like you are. He'd want to be up high, so he could see me better, because that's how he learns. By watching, like your dad."

"Am I like my mum, then?"

"Maybe."

"They're both relentless." Logan's deep voice startles me. "That's not a bad thing, though. Me and Sam are dreamers."

"Oh yeah? What do you dream about, Papa?"

Logan purses his lips. I wonder if he's thinking about how we spent the afternoon. I'm trying not to. It makes me feel so hot inside I can't think straight. And I need my wits. I have twenty-four hours till the last post before Christmas and I'm flat out.

I should be working right now, considering I spent an extended tea break with Logan's cock in my mouth. But the boys asked me to help them decorate their indoor tree before they go back to their mum's tonight, and I couldn't refuse.

Didn't want to. Christmas has passed me by most of my adult life. I forgot how much I like this part.

Also, Logan has a never-ending supply of Mr Kipling mince pies and I am so here for that.

I stuff another one in my mouth while Logan helps Sam hang a wooden reindeer on a bent branch of the plastic Christmas tree. Honestly, this thing looks like it's spent a week on a stag do before it got here. It's fucking brilliant. But observing Sam and Logan reminds me of something else.

Something I left in my jacket pocket at the door.

I excuse myself to the hallway. Logan follows me out, rubbing his stomach, like he has been all afternoon. "You okay there?"

He ignores the question and frowns over my shoulder. "What are you doing?"

"I made something for the boys."

"Why?"

"Because they asked me to."

It's the right answer, apparently. He relaxes a little, but the faint grimace on his face remains, and it draws me to my feet.

I step a little closer to him. "What's wrong?"

"Nothing."

I'm unconvinced. Logan's a big fan of clearing his kids' plates instead of throwing food away, but he didn't eat breakfast this morning and he's pale as fuck. "Can I ask you something?"

"Of course." Logan opens his arms, folding them around me so naturally my next question sounds wrong before I even say it.

"Do you need some space? From me? And what's going on

in here?" I tap the side of his head. "I don't have to be here so much."

"I want you here."

"That's not what I asked."

Logan was already frowning, but it grows deeper now, and he rubs his lips with his big hand. "I don't understand."

There's a day's growth on his jaw. By morning, it'll be gone, ready for his four-day stretch of shifts. I make the most of it while it's there, scratching my blunt nails through it. "You seem stressed."

"I'm okay."

"Sure?"

"No. But it's not you...it's just...*shit*. I'm no good at this."

I wait him out. There's a tiny doubting devil in my gut that's terrified of what he's about to say. But my heart is calm. We're friends. I can take whatever he throws my way as long as he's okay.

Because you love him.

Eh. Leave me alone.

As it happens, Logan doesn't say anything. Billy calls him back to the living room.

I go back to digging in my pockets until I find what I'm looking for.

Then I follow him and pass the paper-wrapped parcel to Sam.

Logan perches on the arm of the couch, watching the boys unwrap their treasure. He still has a hand on his abdomen, half tucked beneath his shirt. It's distracting, but excited noises by the tree pull my attention away.

"Dad, look!" Sam holds the copper decoration to the light. It's a snowflake made from pennies, each one marked with the year he was born.

There's a second one for Billy, identical in all but the colour of the chain threaded through the top. Riotous red for him, blue for his calmer twin.

Billy claims his and thrusts the third and final ornament at his dad. "This is yours."

Logan blinks, somehow half asleep and hyper alert. He takes the largest decoration from Billy and examines it. The snowflake is made from two-pence pieces, some shiny, some not. Some polished by his own hand, some by mine. He didn't notice the other day that he was surrounded by coins with his birth year on, and I forgot to tell him. *Because he fucked you senseless.*

My inner monologue is coming out with some bangers today.

Logan still looks confused. I venture closer to him and explain myself. "Sam asked me if I could make something for your tree that showed you as a family. I think he saw it on a film and he wanted it here."

"Sounds like him." Logan spins the ornament on its chain, sea-green for his killer eyes. "Thank you. They're cool as shit."

"Yeah?"

A genuine smile warms the haze that's hung over him all day. "Yeah. And they'll make me think of you every Christmas, so that can't be bad."

"Remy?" Sam pulls on my sleeve. "What about you?"

I drag my gaze from Logan and give Sam my attention. "What about me?"

Sam frowns, so like his dad, tongue-tied and chewing his lip. He flits his stare between the three decorations and the half-finished tree before it lands on me again. "Can we have one for you, too?"

It takes me a second to compute what he means. Then awkwardness swallows me whole. Sam knows I'm more than friends with his dad. That we kiss by the front door sometimes, fall asleep together on the couch, and share Logan's bed when I stay over. But how do I explain to a seven-year-old none of that means I'll be here next year?

I can't. I'm lost for words and Logan comes to my rescue.

"Remy's too busy to make more stuff for us, kiddo. You're lucky he had time for these."

Sam moves on. The boys hang their decorations and argue over who gets to hang Logan's.

Logan breaks it up. His copper flake is heavier than the others. He places it lower down, stooping with a wince that edges the concern I already feel. Has he hurt himself somehow? His back? His knees? After the year I've had, I should be able to tell, but Logan catches me looking and smooths his expression, coming to me with a soft smile that melts my insides.

He drops his massive hands on my shoulders, the heat of them soothing the ache I'm finding easier and easier to ignore the longer I spend with him. "Are you still wearing that necklace?"

The one that kept hitting you in the face when we fucked last night? I return his grin, unable to stop it stretching wide. "I am. Why?"

"I want to borrow it."

Bemused, I dig the pendant from beneath my clothes.

Logan unhooks it. He draws it away from me and fastens the clasp again before moving to the tree.

I miss his body heat, but curiosity consumes me as Logan wraps my necklace around the branch holding the copper ornament I made for him, winding the weathered leather around it, the penny charm at the base of the snowflake, caught in the glow of the nearest fairy light.

"There." He stands up, this time without cringing, and musses Sam's hair so it's as messy as his brother's. "Remy's with us now."

It's good enough for Sam.

Good enough for *me*.

But what about Logan?

He's fixated on what he's done. On what it means. I want to tell him it doesn't have to mean anything, but I'd be lying.

Because I want it to mean *something*.

I take his hand and tug him away from the tree. "Come to the kitchen with me?"

He doesn't protest as I guide him to the other room. He leans against the counter while I fiddle with the kettle, making tea for him and the coffee I'm going to need to stay up all night working.

If he lets you leave. Some nights he hasn't, and I've been too weak to fight it. I like sleeping with him—in the literal sense. Love it, actually. His big arms. His soft breaths. The way he holds me so tight against him. "You know it's you I want, don't you? Not your bed or your warm house?"

Logan startles, tearing his gaze from the kitchen window. "What?"

"In case you were wondering." I keep my eyes on the coffee mug, stirring harder than it truly requires. "I was on my arse when I came here, but I have money now. I can pay your uncle at the end of the week."

Logan flicks another frown to the window before a dark glare settles on me. "Why the fuck would you think I'm questioning your motives for being with me? I'm the one with a shit ton of complications and a million priorities before I get to you."

"I'm the one living out of a van."

"So? That was your life because you wanted it to be. It's not your fault you got hurt."

"It's not your fault Bec let you think every fucked up thing about your marriage was down to you."

Logan's glower turns biblical. Then it evaporates as though he hasn't got the energy for it. "It's not her fault either. I'm just saying I'm fucking old compared to you. I have this life that

151

sucks me dry sometimes, and it's hard to understand why you'd want a part of it. So no, I'm not standing here wondering if you're fucking me to get a taste of my gas bill."

I'm still stirring the coffee.

I push it away, tracking the swirl in the liquid, the corkscrew of steam it kicks out. His words make sense. At least, they should. But he's neglecting to account for how little any of it matters—the age gap, the wild difference in the lives we've led to get to this point. "I—"

His phone rings. No, it *blares*, making a siren-like sound I've never heard it make before, vibrating on the kitchen counter like it's about to explode.

It changes everything. Logan's face morphs into sharp lines. He snatches his phone from the counter and takes the call, already in motion, leaving the kitchen and me in his wake.

He speaks four words.

The call ends and he runs upstairs.

I don't need to follow him to know he's leaving.

He reappears before I can take a breath, dressed in the sweats and hoodie he wears to the fire station, his phone pressed to his ear again. "Come on, come on. Pick up, Bec."

I get out of his way as he barrels into the living room.

"Boys, get your stuff together. Mum's coming early."

Billy jumps off the couch. "Why?"

"I have to work. Get your bag."

The boys scamper off. Logan curses at his phone before he seems to remember me. "Can I have your coffee?"

I pass it over. "What's happened?"

"Major incident. Fucking knew it. I should've been ready."

"Knew what? I don't understand."

Logan propels me to the window, jabbing a finger to the horizon. To a vicious smoke bloom staining the sky like a mushroom cloud.

"Fucking hell."

"Yup." Logan gulps coffee and opens the fridge. Shuts it and yanks open a cabinet instead. "I need to eat something. It's gonna be a long night."

I help him forage. We find cereal bars and Cadbury's mini rolls.

Logan inhales them, dialling Bec over and over, stress lining his face while I hawk-eye the *horrific* smoke cloud.

"What even is that?"

"The oil depot."

"The what?"

"Storage facility. There's a hundred million litres in that place."

"Shit."

Logan sends me a grim look and calls Bec again. No answer and his hands ball into fists, not seeing the solution that's right in front of him.

I press another cake into his hands. "I can stay until she gets here."

"You have to work too. This isn't your problem."

"What if I want it to be? Why isn't that good enough for you?"

The snap in my voice catches me off guard, ringing out in the kitchen.

Logan has the mini roll halfway to his mouth. He stills. "Good enough? Fuck. No. That's not it. You just shouldn't have to pick up my shit."

"It's not shit and I want to pick it up. Just like you want to feed me and bury me in blankets."

"That's not all I want to do to you." His humour is faint. Absent, almost. But it's there, a flicker of levity that takes the edge off whatever the fuck we're both feeling.

I push the cake towards his mouth. "All I'm saying is I'm right where I want to be, and I *want* to stay with your boys until their mum gets here, for you, and for them. It's not a hardship.

153

It's not *shit*. It's who we are."

Conflict still rages in Logan's gaze, but he's running out of time to argue. The sky in the distance grows darker with every second. Face grave, he scans the horizon, me, and his phone. "I don't know how long I'm going to be. Chances are I'll be gone until tomorrow night."

"It's okay."

"I don't want to leave you like this."

Different day. Same line. "I'm not going anywhere except up the hill."

"Sleep here."

"What?"

"Please." Logan envelops me, abrupt and consuming, swamping me with his whole body. "It's your life, and I respect you so fucking much. I just—"

I press my hand over his mouth. "I'll sleep in your bed and eat all your food." *Whatever he needs*. "If I'm not here when you get back, I'll be up there, working the calories off, okay?"

Logan rips my hand away and kisses me. Hard. Searching. Full of all the things we haven't had time or the words to say. He sweeps his tongue across mine, then pulls back with a sigh. "I know what I want. How I feel. I'm just scared of saying it in case I fuck it up."

"Then don't say it. Let it brew till it's ready. There's no time limit on loving someone."

"You love me, Remy?"

I can't make myself answer. And Logan has to *go*. One last kiss and he's tearing himself away from me.

He says goodbye to his boys and dashes to his car.

I watch him drive away, my heart full.

But it's not just the soul-affirming affection I have for him. It's fear and regret.

I should've told him I love him.

I should've told him a thousand times.

154

Logan

The drive to the station is a blur. I feel like shit in too many ways to contemplate, but there's no time for introspection.

I dump my car and hit the ground running, taking my place in the rig before I've truly taken a breath.

After twenty years in the fire service, ten of them on Blue Watch, it's a process that should feel like old news. Not easy, but familiar. But there's a burn in my belly as we speed towards the city, and it has nothing to do with the apocalyptic fire we're driving into.

I should've told Remy I love him. It makes no fucking sense that I didn't, even before he let slip that he might love me. All the complications I've dreamed up over the past few days—the boys, work, Bec. A dozen other things I don't give a fuck about.

I *love* him.

I trust him.

He'd never hurt my boys. If it all went wrong, we'd survive.

It's funny how perspective can be so reasonable when Armageddon looms in front of you. I can't stop thinking about Remy. About my boys. My brother. But my thoughts quiet as the smoke in the sky grows thicker, the acrid scent of burning oil already muddying the air in the rig.

I'm angry with myself. And...I don't feel fucking well. My stomach aches something unholy, and I'm so tired I can't see straight. But there's something about big fires that alters a firefighter's DNA. We're not like other people. Bec once told me she thought any man who willingly walked into a blaze had a screw loose, and maybe she's right. But as the engine draws closer to the major incident, who I was when I left my house fades away.

Adrenaline kicks in. Tunnel vision descends.

I see my job and nothing else.

We scream into the incident site. It's a fire that's been burning for hours now. There's more engines and firefighters than I've seen in one place for a long time. But I don't think about the scale. I think about our crew and the orders we receive the second we step off the rig.

The incident commander is blunt. "If we can't get the third tank under control, it's going to blow. We've already withdrawn twice, but there's people still unaccounted for. Searches that can't be made until we slow the progression of this blaze."

Progression. Control. It's already a given that we're not putting these fires out.

We suit up and get to work. I follow Galen into the worsening smoke billowing from Tank Three. It's hot. Suffocating. But we train for this every moment we're not fighting other fires, rescuing cats from trees, or scraping bodies from car wrecks.

For hours, we run out covering sprays and lay cooling jets. Could be days for all I know. The smoke is so thick that time becomes something we left behind.

My only certainties are heat, soot, and Galen in front of me. The radio squawking in my ear. The discontented grumble in my belly and the yearning in my soul to be somewhere else.

To be home, where I left my heart with Remy and my boys.

They're not even there. They left hours ago.

I know that. And I know it's likely Remy was humouring me when he promised to spend the night in my bed instead of the freezing workshop. But picturing them all together keeps me upright.

It's nasty o'clock in the morning when we take a break. I chug water while Galen stuffs his face with sandwiches and treats the WRVS have provided.

He waves a jam tart at me.

I almost gag and he frowns.

"Moody. What's up with you?"

"Nothing."

"Dude, you're fucking green."

"Like the Hulk?"

"Nah, like Captain Logan's about to lose his lunch."

I didn't eat lunch. The last thing I'd put in my mouth was seven mini rolls before I'd left the house, knowing I'd need the energy. But that sugar rush is long gone, and I'm flagging. "How long have we got?"

"Officially?" Galen ducks around me to check the time. "Four hours. Reckon they'll keep us another six, though. Green Watch already clocked out."

Already is a relative term. If another watch is done, it means they've *already* put in overtime and it's our turn now.

My stomach churns again. I know the job. Accept it. But the thought of another six hours crawling through that fucking smoke...yup. There it is. I'm gonna puke.

I excuse myself and find a sanitation station. It's not unusual for firefighters to vomit after long shifts in thick smoke, so no one pays much attention. But it's unusual enough for me that Galen follows me.

He's waiting outside the portable cubicle when I shuffle out. "Dodgy curry or a hangover?"

"Neither. Fuck off."

I go to pass him.

He blocks me. "Seriously, dude. What's up? You sick?"

I'm beginning to think I might be. Maybe the kids have brought a bug home. But we haven't got time to worry about it. Our break is up.

I find a grin from somewhere and shove Galen away. "If I was, you in my face wouldn't make it better."

He's unconvinced, but trusts me enough to let it go. I've worked through illness before. We all have. And a shout like this?

I'd have to lose a limb before I walked out on my crew.

We head back in, rinse and repeat our efforts to keep this motherfucking tank whole. For a while we win. Then it becomes clear no matter what we throw at this fire, there's too much fuel at its disposal to save the integrity of the structure around it.

It's going to cave in.

Worse, it might blow.

I see it in the same moment Galen does. Then I hear it—the listing of metal. The creak and crack as it expands more than it was ever meant to.

"Fuck," Galen curses in my ear. "We need out of this hell hole."

An echoing order comes on the radio seconds later, but we're already in motion, dashing for the exit as fast as we can in the smoke-filled pit.

Galen's faster than me, smaller, lighter on his feet. But reversing our positions puts me in front. We drop our equipment. I reach back and grab him, my hand a vice around his arm, and we *run*, hustled out by the swelling heat behind us.

I'm not easy to scare. I've seen too much and survived it. But this smoke—it's so thick. Even through the mask on my face, I can taste it.

My legs grow heavy. Galen shouts, urging me on, and I grit

my teeth, head down, one foot in front of the other. One goal. Get the fuck out.

Maybe that's why I don't see it coming. The tangle of hot metal that rains down on us. Why the ground rushing to meet my face is more of a shock than losing my grip on Galen's arm.

I fall, the impact of the concrete floor ricocheting through my entire body, knocking my mask up my face, exposing my mouth to the poisoned air sucking us dry.

Smoke fills my lungs. I cough, grappling with the mask, losing my bearings.

"Logan!" Galen's shout comes from somewhere above me. "Get up. Keep moving. It's coming down!"

I can't get my fucking mask on. He drops down beside me, his gloved hands as clumsy as mine. We're not panicking—we're not built that way. But we're running out of time.

The mask finds purchase on my face again. I suck clean air, filling my lungs, and fight for my fucking vision instead.

I've lost track of where we are. There's a line somewhere, to guide us out. But I've lost that too.

Galen hauls me up. Behind his mask, his eyes are wide. If I can't get my shit together, we're not getting out.

I grab him again and navigate forward, trusting my instincts to lead us.

Dogged calm overwhelms the fear. We press on, chasing light, and a mystical, distant irony strikes me. Some days, when I'm without my boys, and all I do is work and sleep, I feel like I live in the dark, especially in winter.

But that was before Remy. Before I looked forward to driving home and letting my gaze drift up Firefly Hill, knowing he was there.

And he's waiting for you, remember?

It spurs me on as much as the iron will not to leave my boys without a father. To get my friend and wingman to safety, the way we always have for each other.

One step at a time.

Keep moving.

The exit looms. We're nearly there. My chest is heaving from the nuclear dose of shitty air, but a lightness fills me. We're gonna make it.

A sickening crack smashes into my optimism. It comes from somewhere in the black hole above us, louder, even, than the groaning metal we've left behind. A concrete post smacks the ground in front of me. I manoeuvre around it, but another one slams down, whistling past my fucking face.

I stumble, losing my grip on Galen again. My hands hit the ground. My knees. Hollers of other men reach me, but it's Galen's pained shout that scares the shit out of me.

Fuck.

We're gonna die here and I never told Remy I love him.

Remy

I try to keep my promises. It's why I don't make many, because it's hard to stay rigid when the world keeps turning without you.

The workshop has a better view of the disaster unfolding in the city. I vacillate between horrified staring and hiding in Logan's house, pretending it's not happening. As the night drags on, the second option becomes my favourite.

I sit on the floor in his darkened living room, the only light spilling from the tree in the window, sparkly blue and yellow bulbs, decorations of every colour weighting the branches. The copper snowflakes haunt me, especially the one I made for Logan. He probably didn't realise at the time, but the way he's hung my necklace around it, the leather tangled with the chain, it's going to be a bitch to disentangle. The kind of thing you don't bother with because they look better together anyway.

The symbolism hits me hard and I get to my feet, breaking my resolution to stay away from the window and the raging glow on the horizon. I turned the TV on earlier. Regretted it. In the ten seconds I could swallow all I saw were exhausted, soot-stained firefighters, and I felt fucking sick.

My phone buzzes on the coffee table.

I tear myself away from the horror show in the distance and pick it up.

It's not Logan. Whatever's happening on the ground, I won't hear from him until morning, when he gets to sleep a few hours at the station before his real shift starts.

But it's the next best thing. At least, it would be if I could give Sam and Billy the answers they want as they text me from their mum's phone.

Bec: *is dad home*

Remy: *no. he's not coming back until tomorrow night xx*

Bec: *he mite*

Remy: *he can't. he has another shift. he'll call you when he gets back to the station in the morning.*

I don't know if that's true. It's an assumption I've made based on the man I've grown to love over the last few months. Single dad life isn't one Logan would've chosen for himself, but no one loves anyone as much as he loves those boys.

He's the best fucking dad.

My phone vibrates again.

Bec: *This is Bec. Sorry, the boys woke up and took my phone. I've sent them back to bed.*

Wow. Her grammar is killer. I try to fix mine as I text her back.

Remy: *It's ok. I'm awake anyway.*

Bec: *You're worried.*

Remy: *aren't you?*

Bec: *This is his job. You can't stay up every night he goes to work.*

Bec: *But thank you for being there for the kids. I appreciate it.*

I scowl at the phone, but I don't type another text. Can't when my instinctive—and probably unfair—response isn't something I want Logan's boys to see me say to their mum.

Besides, she's kind of right. The fire at the oil depot is an act

162

of God, but there'll be others. So many others. Am I going to stand at this window for the rest of my life, willing the universe not to take him from me?

If that's what it takes.

I blink at my brain's—no, my heart's, visceral reaction. Visceral *certainty*. I don't know how Logan feels about me for sure, but I know how I feel about him. I *love* him, and for as long as he wants me here, it's where I'll be.

He needs me here now.

I go back to the pile of jewellery I brought down from the workshop. It's finished, but needs packing up, ready for posting tomorrow. I hate this part—faffing with paper and tape. For some inexplicable reason, it's a process I have zero dexterity for. I can unpick the smallest, most delicate chain with untold patience. Give me a roll of Sellotape and I want to hurl the thing at the wall.

Mutilating the parcels keeps me busy, though. The next time I look up, the lights of the tree have become less bright, the darkness outside fading to the mist of an early morning.

Mindful of Logan's *multiple* warnings not to leave tree lights on too long, I get up and turn them off.

I miss their easy glow. Logan's Christmas tree as wild as the one outside. No rhyme or reason. Just unfettered, glorious chaos. But that's the beauty of it. That no one tried to make it anything it wasn't. It's joy and excitement hurled on plastic and I love it.

I *love* it.

Lordy lord, that word is doing some serious heavy lifting tonight. This morning. Whatever. Somewhere upstairs— Logan's room—a radio comes on. It's Gold FM and Chris De Burgh filters down the stairs with the worst Christmas song ever. That maudlin shit about spacemen.

It makes me want to cry and frustration gets the better of me.

I storm to the stairs and thunder up them, past the boys' room and into Logan's.

The bed is still a mess from the afternoon we spent rolling around in it. The window is open, but the imagined scent of sweat and sex hits me. Of Logan. Of me. Of everything we did and everything I want to do with him.

I shut the window and sit on the edge of the bed. Maybe I should make it so Logan has a nicer place to come home to tonight, but I don't move. I'm rooted to this place, staring, unseeing, until my wandering gaze lands on a photograph.

It's Logan and his brother. I've seen it before, or others like it, but it draws me in. How young they are—younger than me. Arms around each other. Faces identical, but so different. Even without the mismatched hair and the heavy tattoos Logan doesn't have, it's easy to see they're different men. Their DNA is the same, but the light in their eyes...it's worlds apart. Logan's twin is as gorgeous as he is, but Logan enchants me. His serious gaze compared to his brother's mirth. The strict set of his shoulders and his ever-present five o'clock shadow.

There's this horrible moment where a true fear that he won't come home overwhelms me. I picture the smoke staining the sky and the red-hot bloom of heat I've been obsessing over and dodging all night long. Logan's a big man. Strong. Capable. It's so easy to imagine nothing could ever knock him down. But that fire...it's huge, and the notion that it could swallow Logan whole chokes me.

Literally. I can't breathe. I rub my chest, trying to force the tight muscles to relax.

It takes a hot minute.

That, and the realisation that I never turned the radio off and now I'm being tortured by East-17.

Fuck that.

I force calm on myself and surge upright to silence Brian

Harvey. My fingers hit the off switch in the same moment a loud knock sounds at the front door.

I'm in motion before it truly registers, dashing for the stairs, Stay Another Day chasing me down.

I skid to a stop in the hallway, reaching for the door as whoever's on the other side jams keys into the lock.

I'm quicker.

I wrench it open and a familiar face stares back at me. A chiselled jaw. Bloodshot sea-green eyes. Dark brows, set in a deep *deep* frown.

He's upset.

It hits me harder than whatever the hell happened to me upstairs, and it takes a second for me to register the blond hair and biker tattoos. The voice that's not quite the one I crave the most.

"Remy?"

"Um." Another dazed blink. "Yeah?"

The man reaches for me, big hand wrapping around my wrist, tugging me out of the house. "I'm Locke. Logan's brother. You need to come with me."

Logan

My body feels like someone's standing on it. I can move my arms and legs. My fingers. My toes. But my torso is a deadweight.

The only reason I know it's there is the sharp shock of pain low down on my right side.

I take a deep breath. Grumble out a curse that booms unnaturally in my ears until another voice cuts me off. Louder. More amused than annoyed.

"Looo-gan. Come on, mate. Time to wake up so you don't look half dead when the mister arrives."

None of those words makes sense. But I recognise Galen's voice enough to force my eyes open and face him.

He's looming over me, one arm in a sling, bruising on the exposed skin peeking out of his collar. Other than that, he looks okay, but he's wearing a hospital gown, so I have to ask.

"What the fuck happened to you?"

"For fuck's sake." He rolls his eyes. "Again? You had an anaesthetic, not a lobotomy."

"What?" I try to sit up.

He puts a hand on my chest, keeping me down. "Easy. You just had surgery, man. No sudden movements."

Nothing he says sinks in. But I heed his advice to stay down. My head spins like I'm on a fucking waltzer and I have no idea why.

I'm not hurt. There's not a scratch on me that I can see and my lungs are sound. So why do I feel like I'm dying?

I take a minute. Suck in another breath and try again to catch my bearings.

Galen's annoying face is the only solid thing in the unfamiliar room. I focus on it. On him, and everything stills.

I'm in a hospital room. In a bed. There's an IV in my arm and I feel nauseous as hell. "What happened?"

Galen waits a moment, as if I'm the one playing the trick. Then he nods and takes a seat in the bedside chair. "Don't fuck about. Last warning or I'm getting the gaffer in here instead. What's the last thing you remember?"

Nothing. I literally can't think of anything except that this is the last place I should be. "I don't know."

"What about the depot shout? You remember that? Spending all night in that fucking pit?"

I think hard, ignoring the head rush, and flickers of reality start to return. The oil depot. The smoke. The heat. And before that, leaving my kids with—

"Fuck. Remy." I lurch upright again and this time, Galen isn't quick enough to stop me with his one uninjured arm. "Whoa. Shit."

The world swims for real this time, and my body rejects it in no uncertain terms. *I'm gonna puke.*

I don't.

Just.

But wow. Galen's warning about sudden movements starts to hit home.

I let him ease me back and raise the head of the bed so I'm not so horizontal.

He scowls down at me. "Stop being so fucking unruly. I told your brother I'd look after you while he was gone."

"Gone? Locke was here? What? Why?"

"One question at a time. And *listen*, okay? Take it in instead of panicking and hurling your guts up. Christ, you didn't eat anything all night. I don't know how there's anything left inside you."

I don't understand. Remy ambushes my brain again. I fight the urge to battle whatever the hell has happened to my body, but Galen finally seems to take me seriously.

He puts his hand on my arm. We're good friends. Wingmen in the field. But it's a weird thing for him to do. *Did I lose a fucking limb?*

I check, wriggling my fingers and toes again. Nope. All still there.

Remy.

Fuck. I never told him I love him.

That raw feeling comes flooding back.

Galen grips my arm harder. "The oil depot. You remember, right?"

I nod. Slowly. "We were coming out?"

"Yup. That's it. Five metres from the cordon and the fucking apex collapsed. I got trapped by a post. You pulled your Goliath trick and got me out, but you hit the deck after. Thought you'd taken a hit we couldn't see, but turns out your appendix blew up."

"My...appendix?"

Galen nods. "Don't worry, they took it out already. That's why you feel so upside down. Also, you got some good drugs in your veins. Probably why you can't remember the first six times we've had this conversation."

I truly can't. But I don't care. I let the information sink in, piece by piece. Let it merge with the rest of me that's starting to reach land. "I left the boys with Remy."

168

"That was yesterday, mate."

"Yesterday." Shit. "What time is it?"

"Seven."

"In the morning?"

Galen nods. "The boys are with Bec. It's the first call Locke made when the gaffer reached him."

Locke. My brother. My fucking twin. I haven't asked about him because I don't need to. He's not here. Which means he's doing something else to have my back. "Remy—"

"On his way." Amusement returns to Galen's face. "That's where your better-looking brother went. To fetch this dude you can't stop talking about."

"Locke went to get Remy?" My pulse settles. I know my kids are safe with Bec. But I need my brother. I *need* Remy. Cos I have to tell him. "I have to tell him I love him."

Galen nods. "Rightio. Maybe then you'll stop telling me."

The next time I wake up, everything's different. I know where I am: the hospital. And I have a loose idea how I got here. Also, I feel fucking different. Less unhinged. And there's a heavenly sensation dancing up and down my forearm. Fingertips buzzing with heat. Laced with a sense of *right* that has my eyes opening with the beginnings of a smile on my face.

Remy grins back at me. "Afternoon."

"Is it?" I wince at the hoarseness in my voice. The scratch in my throat. "It was sparrow's fart last time I checked."

"Good. That means you've been resting. How'd you feel now? Better?"

"Better than what?"

"Better than working a twelve-hour shift with a burst appendix." Remy's grin fades a little. "It could've killed you."

"Didn't though, did it?"

169

"Lucky for me, no." Remy skates his fingers down my arms again. Goosebumps prickle my skin and his humour disappears for real. "You cold?"

"It's just you."

"I'm not cold."

"Not what I meant."

Remy slow blinks into a nod. "Glad you're still feeling the magic, Papa. You've been asleep so long I was worried you'd forget me."

"Really?"

"No. But I missed you."

"I love you."

"Huh?" Remy's head jerks up. He's perched on the edge of the bed, my hand in his lap, our fingers entwined as he tickles alchemy into my forearm.

His surprise is cute.

And unacceptable. I wrap my spare arm around myself and force myself a little more upright. Unlike Galen, Remy doesn't stop me. He's too busy wide-eyeing me like I just told him the earth is fucking flat.

I make a grab for him.

Miss.

He steadies me and leans close enough that I find his shoulder, his neck, and finally his jaw, my thumb finding its favourite place on his high cheekbone.

"Listen, I know I'm a mess right now, and I fucked up before I left yesterday, or whenever the hell that was, but I *love* you, and I should've fucking told you before I walked out on you to work a job like that."

Remy's coffee bean eyes remain like saucers. "That the only reason? The apocalypse fire down the hill?"

"Fuck, no. I should've told you when I met you."

Remy laughs, his beautiful face lighting up. "You knew it then? In that field in Leicester?"

"Not up here." I drum my fingertips on his temple. "But I felt it everywhere else."

His humour crystallises and he pries my hand from his jaw, lacing our fingers together. "I wasn't sure if you did—feel it, I mean. It was so earth-shifting for me, and so much happened after that, it was hard to believe it was real. Some days, I thought I'd dreamt you up."

"Me too. I mean, I dreamed of you. Not myself."

"Fair enough. How do you feel now? Better than you did before?"

"Before what?"

"Before you left for work yesterday. That knock on the door scared the shit out of me, but when they told me what happened, it made sense. You'd been weird all day."

I think on that, piecing together what I remember from the last time Remy was this close to me. "Was the sex weird?"

"No, Papa. Just you." Remy starts to laugh, but he's not the loudest in the room.

A deep chuckle comes from the other side of the bed, and I whip my head around to find the *highly* amused face of my brother. My *twin*. My best friend and other half.

The biggest dickhead I've ever met, who's killing himself trying to contain his laughter.

Fucking hell. "How long have you been there?"

Locke wheezes, tears cresting his eyes. "The whole time, bro. Never knew you were such a poet."

"Fuck off."

"Nope. You nearly died. That means I get a pass on witnessing your emotional fuckery for the next three days."

"Three days?"

"That's how long you have to stay," Remy supplies. "You had open surgery, not the keyhole one."

"Because your appendix *burst*," Locke adds, in case I'm not getting the picture.

I am. I just don't care. It was broken, now it's gone. Worrying about it is as pointless as pretending I give a fuck my brother heard me declare my undying love for Remy. Three days, though? A sigh escapes me. There goes my grand plans to be a real dad at Christmas.

Locke rises from the seat I hadn't noticed him occupying.

Remy's gaze flits between us and he stands too, disentangling his hand from mine. "I'll be back in a sec."

Anxiety rears up in me.

Remy sees and kisses my cheek. "Just giving you a moment with your brother. I'll be back, I promise."

His words are a whisper, but they settle me, and I let him go, keeping my gaze on him until the door shuts behind him.

Then I face my brother and another wave of peace washes over me. I love Remy, and my boys are my world. But Locke. He's been my soul my whole fucking life.

He gives me a gentle hug, smelling of cigarettes and diesel. Then he drops his big palm on top of my head, like we always do when one of us is down. "Papa?"

"Piss off. I like it."

"I can tell."

"Oh yeah?"

"Yeah." Locke musses my hair, then reclaims his hand. "And I don't blame you. He's the prettiest bloke I've ever seen—"

"It's not about that."

"I know. If you'd let me finish, I'd have said so."

"Good." I settle back on the bed, tired, despite the fact I've apparently been asleep forever.

Locke gives me a second, letting me scan the room and take in my surroundings properly. There's not much to it. Just a bed, a couple of chairs, and some tinsel hanging off the door handle.

"Is it Christmas Eve tomorrow?" He says suddenly.

Least, it feels that way to me. "Maybe?"

"I think it is. You were going to be working, right?"

"Think so." Work is the last thing on my mind, though it suddenly dawns on me that the whole station probably knows about Remy now.

Locke reads my frown like a boss. "Chill. No one gives a fuck about stuff like that anymore. It's not the eighties."

"It's not, is it?"

"No. Besides, you literally turned into the Hulk to save Galen's life. Any man on the job knows that's worth more than anything."

"Or woman."

Locke snorts. "Women don't need such basic things explained to them."

I chew on that, drifting a little, until I notice my brother has sobered to a point he rarely bothers to reach. "What's the matter?"

Locke puts his hand on my head again. "It's just hitting me that if you'd been home alone when you went down, you'd be dead."

"Why are you thinking about that?"

"Cos I'm human, bro. And I love you. I don't know what I'd do if anything happened to you."

"Nothing's happening to me." It's a conversation we've had before, so many times, in reverse too. We both know the words are hollow, but we say them anyway. It is what it is. "If it's any consolation," I say, when Locke's stopped glowering at me like I'm about to expire. "I don't plan on being home alone much anymore."

"Yeah, I got that. You really love him, eh?"

I nod. "I've never felt this way about anyone."

"Was it a thunderbolt?"

"I think it was." My eyes grow heavy and my brother laughs at me. I know he's going to leave soon, but it's okay. We don't have to live in each other's pockets to keep our bond.

Pretty sure I fall asleep. When I'm next aware of my

surroundings again, Locke is gone, and Remy is back, his smile so fucking sweet I have to touch it to be sure I'm awake.

He laughs at me too, opening his lush mouth to bite my fingers.

The sensation sends a jolt of energy to my veins, letting me know I've passed another milestone in finding myself again. "Did Locke leave?"

Remy shakes his head. "His friend took him to get some food."

"What friend?"

"Another hot dude with tats. I think they told me his name, but that was before I saw you, so I wasn't really listening."

My brother has lots of friends with ink. Truth be told, it could be anyone, but bringing them here tells me that it's someone who matters. I file it away to think about later. Focus on Remy as he hops down from the bed and bends to retie his bootlace. As he comes upright, I find myself lost in the easy elegance of his movements. The lightness. Looking at him, the colour in his cheeks, the gaunt pallor nowhere in sight, he's more the angel I met in the summer than ever.

He catches me staring. "What?"

"You look well," I blurt. "It's nice."

Remy sits on the edge of the bed again. "There's a secret to that, you know."

"Oh yeah? What's that?"

"I have this tall, dark, and handsome bloke feeding me three times a day. Keeping me warm at night. I'm sorry I implied that didn't mean anything yesterday, because it does. It means a lot that you did that for me, and I appreciate it more than you know."

"Do you love me, Remy?" There's an echo in my head, as if I've uttered those words before, but I don't remember his response. "You don't have to answer that."

Remy laughs. A real, tip-his-head-back belly laugh. "You're

taking the piss, right? Of course I love you. Everything you've said in this room—fuck, right back at you a thousand, million times. I know it's fast, and it's kind of mad, but it's special, Papa. What we've found, and I'm so happy you feel that too."

Happy. It suits him. That smile. God, it's everything. I'm still messy and tired, but so was he when he pulled up that workshop door all those weeks ago. And maybe that's what love is. Messy. Like those coins Remy spends all day toiling over. None of them are perfect, but together they make something beautiful.

I pull him as close as I can without wrenching the stitches in my belly. "I know it wasn't my shitty house that attracted you to me. But I just want to say, thank you for fixing everything. I'd never have got round to it on my own."

Remy relaxes into my wobbly embrace, hair tickling my nose. "Maybe next time something breaks, we'll fix it together."

Remy

Three weeks later...

Christmas in January. It's a thing. The tree is still in the living room window. The one outside remains lit up like Heathrow runway and there's no one around to see it except us at the top of Firefly Hill.

There's even a turkey in the oven, though neither me or Logan has a clue how long it should stay there.

"If we fuck it up, there's sausages in the freezer."

Logan says this from behind me, his arms clamped around my waist, his chin on my head. It's his favourite place to be at the moment.

"We won't fuck it up," I say absently. I'm cutting up Brussel sprouts I'm pretty sure no one will eat, but Logan wants them anyway. "There's Bisto, right? That fixes everything."

Logan hums into my neck. His soft lips and rough jaw make my blood pump a little harder, but I dampen it down. He's smashing recovery like it's an Olympic sport. Aside from a few loopy days in hospital, and a couple of extra naps, it's hard to tell anything happened to him. But no sex. Doctor's orders are not to strain his abdomen and the kind of fucking Logan's so good at?

176

Yeah. Not happening.

A few hours later, we eat Christmas dinner at Logan's kitchen table with his brother on FaceTime, his hot biker friend in the background. No one eats the sprouts. But we laugh a lot, so who the fuck cares?

Logan's the best Christmas dad. I'd wish he were mine if that wasn't totally fucking weird.

He washes up with the boys. I collect the detritus from "Christmas Morning" littering the living room floor. Wrapping paper. Silly string. Foil from the chocolate coins the boys ate for breakfast.

I gather the scraps of silver tissue paper from the gift Logan gave me. The house key that hangs around my neck on weathered leather he must've swiped from the workshop.

"I'm not asking you to move in—I know you're not there yet. But consider it a permanent invitation to be here whenever you want to be, because we want you here all the time."

Not there yet. It's a phrase I don't like, but he's so right. I want to spend every waking moment with Logan, but I can't move in with him. Not when I have sixty quid in my PayPal account and no idea if the next few months are going to change that.

That he knows without me telling him makes me love him even more.

"Remy?" Sam pulls on my sleeve.

I abandon the bin bag I'm filling and give him my full attention. "What's up?"

"Can we play with the rope thing now?"

Rope thing. He means the poi I gave the boys for Christmas, knowing full well the sight of them would make their firefighter dad wince.

"I can't let my kids play with literal fire."

I know that. It's why I gave them the LED set I've never had the patience to use. Also, so they can dance in the rain, like I did, the day I met Logan.

It's raining now, the snow from December long gone. That light drizzle that somehow still soaks a man to the skin. "You'll have to ask your dad if he's okay with you getting wet."

"It's fine." Logan's gruff voice comes from the doorway, but I don't turn around. As much as I love him, if Sam and Billy want my attention, they get it first.

We head outside. Logan sits on the porch step, under cover and taking a rest, while I show the boys how to throw their new toys around. The LED lights are bright and they cast patterns in the night sky. Can't lie and pretend I don't prefer the wildness of open flame, but I'd forgotten how good it feels to move my body like this. To stretch and spin. Falling in love with Logan brought me back to life. But this, with his magical little boys, reminds me I never stopped living.

It's late by the time Logan calls us inside. He packs the boys upstairs to brush their teeth and get ready for bed.

The second they're out of sight, he pins me to the wall. "You fucker."

He swallows my answer with the kind of kiss I'm only built for when we're *alone*. Because *he's* the fucker and I'm at his mercy, letting him steal every ounce of breath in my lungs.

"I don't know what you mean," I protest when we break for air.

Logan dead-eyes me. "You were dancing like that when I first saw you. For, like, five minutes. Watching you do it tonight for two *fucking hours* has just about killed me."

"It's not a bad way to go." The joke is a hard reach. I'm still reeling that he nearly died from something as simple as appendicitis. And that's not even considering the heroic brush with death him and Galen survived before that.

But I do reach it. I have to. Logan's a firefighter. A real-life superhero for any soul who needs him.

I'm just lucky he wants to be mine.

And that he's out of his mind with whatever watching me chuck LED poi around has done to him.

He's too worked up to put the boys to bed.

I do it and they act like it's the most exciting thing to ever happen to them.

Billy pulls me closer to his bunk. "You'll be here in the morning, won't you?"

"Yup."

"Cos you're sleeping over with Dad?"

"Yup."

"He likes that."

"I like it too. Go to sleep, yeah? Then the morning will be here quicker."

I shut their door and pad back downstairs.

Logan is on the couch, slouched low, drinking a beer. He's wearing those faded jeans that are moulded to his perfect body. An old T-shirt that's riding up, revealing his furred, chiselled abs, and the fresh scar on the righthand side of his belly.

It's kinda hot. At least, it will be when it's healed enough that seeing him poured onto the couch like that is something I can act on.

Logan crooks two fingers and beckons me closer.

I plant my feet on the floor three feet away from him. "Nope. No strenuous activity, remember?"

"There's nothing strenuous about wanting you."

"Want me from over there then."

"*Remy.*"

God. He has this way of saying my name.

It overwhelms my autonomy and I'm standing between his legs before I have a clue what I'm doing.

He sits up slightly, hands on my thighs, sliding them up to my hips, fingers dipping into the waistband of the black cotton trousers I swapped for my rain-damp jeans.

I don't stop him as he tugs them down, pulling me closer so he can kiss my stomach.

I'm already half hard. His hot breath on my skin? Yeah. I'm here for that. "Careful," I whisper. "It's no fun if you hurt yourself."

Logan hums a laugh. "Not gonna happen."

He takes me in his mouth, his lips wrapped around my cock, tongue ghosting up and down. *Damn*, he sucks my dick the same way he fucks me. Hot and relentless. A fairground ride that reaches too many peaks for me to count.

And he loves it when we have to be quiet. The challenge of drawing silenced groans from me.

There's too many of those to count too.

I don't try.

I give in and let Logan take me as high as he wants before he hurls me off the edge. I grip his hair and pump my hips, chasing the bliss he's gifting me, hunched over, breathing ragged.

He scrapes his teeth along my length and I'm done. Knee braced on the couch, I come hard into his waiting mouth.

He's so pleased with himself. His satisfied grin is light, shaving the years from his handsome face. He's also pent up as hell, a scandalous bulge in his jeans.

When I've caught my breath, I pop the buttons, setting him free. No underwear. Just his massive dick jutting out from his strong body, heat radiating from every pore. "I should make you wait for ambushing me like that."

Logan smirks. "Are you gonna?"

No. "Maybe."

He knows I'm lying. I've never been so into someone, and every week that goes by, the connection we share, the current, it runs hotter and hotter.

I won't make him wait.

Because I can't.

I make him come with my mouth, working him with my fist

at the same time, watching him fight to keep his hips still and the pressure off his healing abdomen.

The strain of it is fucking beautiful. His clenched jaw. The arch of his throat as he throws his head back, a silent groan shaping his lips.

His big thighs trembling.

It makes me want to explore more of him. And one day I will. Because that's what I want. What *he* wants. A permanence that becomes our forever.

He's knackered.

We clean up and creep upstairs. Logan curves around me, one hand on my hip, the other tangled in my hair. In the night, he'll throw a leg over me, pinning me down, and I *love* that. The weight of him. His solid warmth. The way he holds me like he's been waiting for me his whole life.

I find the hand on my hip and squeeze it. "Hey, Papa?"

"Yeah?"

"Merry Christmas."

Logan laughs, sleepy and content. "Merry fucking Christmas."

Logan

Summer Now

Billy and Sam tear up the hill, pumping their legs on their bikes. I follow more sedately. I'm strong enough to pedal like a man possessed, but the summer sun beating on my bare back has got me feeling lazy.

Can't deny I'm as excited as they are to get to the top of Firefly Hill, though. It's late afternoon and the heat is starting to mellow. There's no smoke in the sky, but I know he's there.

Remy.

My kids' best friend and the love of my fucking life.

He hears us coming, naturally. Billy hollers so loud my brother can probably hear him in Devon.

I slow my lackadaisical pace even more, watching Remy emerge from the workshop and greet my noisy kids like they're his whole fucking world.

Like me, he's shirtless, dressed just in those cotton trousers he wears all year round.

I have new appreciation for them now the warmer months are here. They hang low on his hips, the sun bouncing off his inked skin, hair blond like a fucking halo.

And his smile. It's still hard to believe he's real, until he turns that mile-wide grin on me and the shot to my heart is so intense I wobble on my bike.

Bloody hell.

I make it to the summit without breaking my neck.

Remy has already put the boys to work, a reality they take so much better from him than they ever do from me or their mum.

Sam is polishing a copper tabletop, the fourth Remy's made this year.

Billy is emptying Remy's van—a sight I never thought I'd see. Remy's old Transit is an Aladdin's cave of weirdness. Hand to God, I've never seen him duck into the back of that thing and not reappear with something crazy.

Case in point: my son is currently stacking wooden stilts against the workshop door.

"You don't need them this weekend?" I wonder as I roll to a stop.

Remy glances at them. "They're not mine. I'm looking after them for a clown I met three years ago and haven't seen since."

Sounds about right. Getting to know Remy better has taught me that he has many, *many* acquaintances, but few real friends. He keeps most people at arm's length.

I'm one of the lucky ones.

My boys too.

My brother. It's a rare call now that Locke doesn't ask to speak to Remy too.

I miss my brother. An old wound, but with Remy in my life, it hurts less.

I lean my bike next to the stilts and peer into the back of Remy's van. It's mostly empty, bar the mattress that no longer lives on the workshop floor, and a few other things. "Huh. It's nicer than I thought."

"Having second thoughts about kipping in here with me?"

"Never." I make a grab for Remy as he drifts close enough

for me to reach. Find purchase on his waist and haul him in. "Just wondering if I'll fit."

"The mattress is the same size as your bed."

Our bed. But...alas, no. Despite spending every night beside me, and keeping it warm when I'm on shift, Remy still doesn't officially live with us. He has money now. A steady income from his Etsy business. He pays for every food shop that lands in my kitchen cupboards and sneaks utility bills out of my house to pay them at the Post Office before I can.

But because he's a stubborn motherfucker, he still calls the cottage *your house, Papa* and gets his post delivered to the workshop, and I can't do a thing about it.

We take the boys home. Have dinner and fall asleep on the couch. At least, I do. It's my favourite thing, to doze in front of bullshit telly while Remy plays with my hair.

One of them, anyway.

The next morning, I deliver the boys back to Bec and climb into Remy's dodgy Transit. It's packed and ready to go.

"No bitching about my driving." He shoots me a droll grin. "You're off-duty all weekend."

I'll never be off-duty when it comes to giving a shit about him. "It's not your driving I worry about. It's everyone else's."

"Out of your hands, Papa. Just relax."

Easier said than done, but we're leaving my world and going back to Remy's, to festival life, so I can watch him dance with fire and pretend I'm absolutely not monitoring every fire marshal in sight. As if I can death glare them into taking their job seriously.

The festival isn't one I've heard of. By day it seems pretty tame. Then night falls and I help Remy smear glitter on his skin and dunk his wild hair in fire retardant.

He dances away from me, twirling his flaming poi over his head, moving faster and faster, his steps so swift and free under the summer stars that he's more otherworldly than ever.

I sit on the dry grass, drinking spiced rum from a bamboo bottle. In the air, I smell weed and mischief. To be honest, this place smells like sex, but that might just be me. Alone with Remy, away from work and parenthood, it's all I can think about. My body is as hot as the sparks bursting over his head.

I want him so fucking much.

The night draws on. I'm not drunk by the time Remy returns to my side for good, but I'm merrier than when he left me.

Smoke clings to his skin, a scent that sets my teeth on edge, but on Remy, it just makes me simmer with a desire that spins my head.

He drops his poi and straddles me, right there in the field, not giving a fuck about the people around us.

I don't give a fuck either. As the night's gone on, it's become more clear that this isn't a family event. Over Remy's shoulder, I can literally see a couple having sex beneath an old oak tree.

If I had eyes for anyone but Remy, I'd stare. But he's on me, kissing the shit out of me, glitter from his skin making my torso sparkle too.

He pushes me, toppling me onto my back. "It's so hard to dance for anyone but you."

"Yeah?" I bite his lush bottom lip. "Why's that?"

"Papa, you know why."

I do. I feel it in every inch of his lean, wired body. In his every touch. I let him pin me to the grass until I know we have to move before we do something I'm not comfortable with the rest of the festival seeing.

I mean, they can gawp at my naked body as much as they like.

But Remy is mine.

We wind up in the back of the van. The doors are open, nothing but woodland beyond it. The air still smells like sex, and if I strain my ears, I hear other people going at it. But Remy is stripping the few clothes he's wearing, so I don't give a shit.

He stretches out beneath me, naked and beautiful. I push inside him, making his eyes roll and his toes curl, spreading his legs wide, making room for my big body.

I fuck him slowly, making the most of the upper hand I have while he's like this.

But it's not long before his devilish hands wander, the prostate massager he's been teasing me with for days already lubed and ready.

He loves this.

So do I.

Remy presses it against me, sliding it inside, careful. Respectful. All the while I'm still fucking him, though my rhythm falters as pressure and vibrations rock my senses.

A harsh breath escapes me.

Fucking hell.

I thought I was good at sex, but Remy—fuck. He has this extra level that blows my mind. Sends me reeling each and every time, every muscle stretched to that eye-rolling point of perfect near pain.

The toy inside me buzzes, low and persistent. I grip Remy's leg, lifting it higher. He collapses on his back again, half laughing.

Half moaning with a potent *need* that lights me on fire.

I start moving again, fucking him deep and slow, still not giving a solitary shite that the van doors are wide open, foxes and owls probably watching us bang. Tunnel vision descends. I'm not anyone's dad. I'm not a firefighter with a deathly blaze bearing down on me. This, right here. It's just him and me climbing to an oblivion that's going to shatter us and put us back together before we catch our breaths.

The massager hammers my nerves. Each thrust a new burst of sensation.

Another ragged breath scratches out of me, and I dig my fingers into Remy's elegant leg. "Fuck. I'm gonna—"

"*Logan.*" Remy's shaking, his whole body alive with what we share. Sometimes he calls me *Papa* during sex and it's next-level hilarious.

But I'm so beyond humour right now, and the way he says my name pushes me deeper into him.

We reach another plane. A climax rips through him, and I savour every second of it. Every fucking moan, fighting my own soul-splitting release, climbing higher and higher until I have nowhere to go.

I thrust harder, the massager tormenting me with torturous pleasure.

Then I come, mind-numbing and hard, exploding inside Remy with nothing between us but pure fucking love.

It takes a moment for awareness to reach me again.

Remy is still catching his breath.

I reach back and pull the toy out of me, tossing it... somewhere. Then I ease back from Remy. Help him clean up. Gaze at him, blissed out warmth flaring between us.

Happiness transcends. It's still an emotion I'm getting used to. Him too. But everything's easier together. Even wedging my lumbering frame into the back of this fucking van.

I lie next to him, picking grass and who knows what out of his hair. I find a legit feather.

"I was saving that," he murmurs.

"For what? Nest building?"

"You're the nester, Papa."

He's half asleep, but something expands in me that I can't ignore. A burgeoning need that has nothing to do with the fact that we're both naked to the balmy summer breeze. "It's time, Rem."

He blinks, startled by the force in my voice. "Huh? What is?"

"Live with us. Properly. *Officially*. I want our home to belong to both of us."

"You're not giving me your house."

"It's not mine to give you. I have a mortgage, remember? So really, all I'm trying to give you is a colossal debt."

And a massive change to his lifestyle. Before me, Remy lived day to day, month to month, a life without roots. I can't offer him that.

I don't want to.

I don't *need* to. I know me and the boys are enough for him.

With Remy, the trouble has always been he doesn't believe he's enough for us.

I nuzzle his neck, breathing him in. "I love you. Just...be with us, please?"

It's a different question to the one about house deeds and utility bills. The one where I write his name on the list of people allowed to collect my sons from school. But in this moment, to me, it's all the same.

In the murky light of the rusty old van, Remy frowns, like he always does when this comes up. "Are you sure you really want that? I'm shit with money."

"How do you figure that? You never spend any."

"My work's insecure. It could evaporate overnight."

"So? It's not about the money. It's about us—Rem, we're a family."

His brown eyes redden. For a heart-stopping moment, I fear he's about to refute that claim.

Then he sighs, his ethereal smile sliding back into place. "All right then. Sign me up."

Too many emotions hit me to process. I laugh and kiss him, but he's already halfway back to sinking into sleep. I'm losing him, but not really. The night might be dark, but with Remy, it never feels that way.

The beginning or the end, it doesn't matter. Every summer,

every winter. Every Christmas, every spring. He's my story. He's my fucking heart.

And I'm the luckiest man in the world.

Thank you so much for reading Christmas On Firefly Hill. After a year spent writing gritty biker books, Logan and Remi were a joy to discover.

Sign up for my newsletter here.

And please consider my Patreon. All my boys end up there eventually, and I think these two, given their connection to the Rebel Kings MC, will feature quite a lot in the coming year. Sign up HERE.

Interested in Locke? Then I highly recommend starting the Rebel Kings MC series. His book is **Unholy Trinit**y, but he features as a side character from book 3, and he's honestly one of my favourites. You can check out the entire series HERE.

LOOKING FOR MORE CHRISTMAS ROMANCE? Check out **The Christmas Collection**. Three bestselling MM holiday romance novels, featuring exclusive bonus scenes for each book, and lots of Rebel Kings cameos.

Other Holiday Titles

Check them out on my Amazon author page <3

About the Author

Right now, Instagram is the best way to keep up with Garrett. Click on the icon below to follow, or search @garrett_leigh

Bonus Material available for all books on Garrett's Patreon account. Includes short stories from Misfits, Slide, Strays, What Remains, Dream, and much more. Sign up here: https://www.patreon.com/garrettleigh

Facebook Fan Group, Garrett's Den.

Garrett is also an award winning cover artist, taking the silver medal at the Benjamin Franklin Book Awards in 2016. She designs for various publishing houses and independent authors at https://www.blackjazzdesign.com

Connect with Garrett
www.garrettleigh.com

Also by Garrett Leigh

Info for all my books can be found on my website: http://www.
garrettleigh.com